Midnight of Ashes

Dragons of Ember Hollow

Tessa Hale

Cover Design: Hang Le
Paperback Formatting: Champagne Book Design

Midnight of Ashes

CHAPTER ONE

Hayden

PAIN. IT WAS THE ONLY THING THAT EXISTED. A FIERY inferno burning me from the inside out.

Some part of me was aware of hitting the ground. The crash into the hard cement was nothing compared to the agony inside my chest.

My body rolled, my focus aiming skyward. The sky was so beautiful. Completely clear. Stars shining.

Those stars wavered a bit, seeming to blink in and out.

My hearing came back in a whoosh. There were shouts. Footsteps pounded against the pavement.

And then Easton's face filled my vision.

God, he was beautiful. Even knowing how much he hated me, I couldn't help that tug toward him. Couldn't help drinking in that beauty.

His man bun was slightly askew now. Strands of that light brown dipped in gold fell across his face. A face that had gone chalky pale. His usually tanned skin was an unnatural shade of white.

"Hayden," Easton croaked.

I wanted to say something back. To tell him it would be okay. But my mouth couldn't form the words. My tongue felt thick and sluggish, impossible to move.

Easton's hands hovered over me, as if they didn't know what to do. And then finally, he pushed down on my chest.

It wasn't until his palms connected with my torso that I realized the pain had dulled. Or maybe I had been in shock? But I wasn't anymore.

A fresh wave of agony swept over me. The fire was back, eating away at me from the inside out. I couldn't help it, I screamed.

Easton let loose a string of curses. "I'm sorry. I'm so fucking sorry. I have to. I have to hurt you."

The shock took hold again, the worst of the pain numbing. The stars above me flickered, and my eyelids fluttered along with them.

Easton pushed harder on my chest. "No. Don't close your eyes, Hayden. Stay with me."

Why did Easton care? He didn't want me here. Maybe it would just be easier if I slipped away.

"Please," he begged.

My eyes opened again, trying to understand the pleading in his voice.

Easton's eyes shimmered in the moonlight. "Why?" he rasped. "Why the hell would you do that?"

I wanted to tell him that he mattered. Even when he was an asshole. But I couldn't get the words out.

A single tear slid free from his eye, falling and splashing onto my cheek.

Shouts sounded. I couldn't tell how far away they were, couldn't discern the voices over the ringing in my ears. Easton yelled something back, but it wasn't threatening. It had to be the guys.

New faces hovered above me, and I tried to make them out. Through the blur of my vision, I recognized Knox. He crouched next to me, taking my hand.

"Hayden," he whispered, so much pain in that one word.

Maddox barked something at Easton, who immediately jerked back. Easton stood, staring down at his hands. Hands covered in blood. My blood.

Then Maddox's face filled my vision. "I'm so sorry, Mo Ghràidh. This is going to hurt like hell."

He didn't wait for me to attempt an answer; he simply shoved something into my chest. If I'd still had the ability to scream, the sound would've been wrenched from my throat. But I didn't. It was as if there was only a small part of me that could even feel the pain.

If I'd been with it, I would've recognized that Maddox was packing my wound, trying to stop the bleeding until help arrived.

My mouth wanted to pull down in a frown. Would help even come? I'd been hit with a blast of dragon fire. I didn't know if there was any coming back from that.

"Press here," Maddox ordered Knox.

Knox's face blanched, but he nodded. He pressed down on the gauze. I didn't feel any pain at the contact. That had to be bad. It should hurt like the fires of hell.

"Cáel, the IV," Maddox barked.

That was when I saw my Viking warrior for the first time. He struggled to breathe as he pawed through a medical bag, finally shoving some sort of tubing and a sealed packet to Maddox.

His eyes came to me. The pale blue was almost absent of color now. There was so much pain there. And more than that, terror.

The urge to comfort him was so strong. I thought it might be enough to give me the strength to get up off the pavement and simply wrap my arms around him. But it wasn't.

"Small pinch," Maddox whispered.

That hurt. The tenderness in Mad's voice. The way he was still explaining everything he was doing, even though I knew I was halfway gone.

I didn't feel the needle go into my skin, didn't feel it when he inserted the thin tube. But I did feel a wash of cool liquid hit my veins. Drugs. Something to ease the agony.

Maddox didn't know I'd already gone numb, and this was the only thing he could do to help. The world went a little blurrier.

Cillian's large form hovered above him. "They'll be here in under five minutes."

Maddox looked up at him, his expression going completely blank. "I don't know if she'll make it that long."

CHAPTER TWO

Easton

I COULDN'T STOP STARING DOWN AT MY HANDS. IT WASN'T AS if they had never been covered in blood before. They'd been stained this reddish-brown more times than I could count. But it was like I'd never experienced it before. Because it was *her*.

Guilt swamped me. But it wasn't a passive, sluggish emotion. This guilt was brutal, surging through my veins and burning everything in its path. It had gone completely feral.

Even after everything I'd done, especially tonight, Hayden had stepped into the path of dragon fire for me.

Why?

The question swirled round and round in my brain.

"You're going to make her hold on," Cillian growled.

The alpha waves in his voice jerked me out of my haze. Cillian was glaring down at Maddox, who was working on Hayden. Mad had packed her chest full of gauze and inserted an IV. God, I hoped he'd given her something to take the edge off.

I'd hear Hayden's scream when I tried to stop her bleeding for the rest of my life.

"I'm doing everything I can," Maddox said. His voice was completely empty, void of all emotion. As if he'd gone dead inside.

"Mad!" Knox shouted, panic digging into his tone. "I don't think she's breathing."

Maddox cursed, bending so that he was hovering over her. "We need to start CPR."

But Hayden's chest was already shredded. I didn't think CPR was going to do a damn thing to help. Still, Maddox began compressions while Knox executed rescue breaths.

Cáel's massive form filled my vision. "You. This is on you." He shoved me hard, but I didn't try to stop him. "This is what you wanted from the beginning. Are you happy now?"

Cillian grabbed him by the back of the shirt, tugging him back before his fist could connect with my face. But I wished our alpha hadn't stopped him. I wished Cáel's fist would've crushed my jaw. Then maybe I'd have a slight distraction from the agony swirling in my chest.

"Get a hold of yourself. This is the last thing we need," Cillian barked.

Sirens sounded. I caught the flash of lights in the distance.

I knew Cillian would've called our horde's ambulance. We had it for coverage. If a dragon shifter was injured, there was always a chance they could transform without meaning to. Our ambulance was stocked with a drug that prevented the shift and had medical supplies that were shifter specific.

Every minute or so, Maddox would order Knox to "breathe". I couldn't take the command, what it meant. A fresh wave of anguish ripped through me each time.

The ambulance squealed to a stop, and two horde members jumped out. Even they, who had seen more than their fair share of injuries, faltered at the sight of Hayden. They knew who she was to my bond mates. Knew what this could mean.

They hurried over with some sort of machine, connecting pads to Hayden's chest.

"Clear," Gretchen ordered.

Everyone moved back.

Hayden's body jerked in an unnatural motion. I wanted to turn away, but I couldn't.

Gretchen pressed her fingers to Hayden's neck and gritted her teeth. "Clear."

Hayden's body jerked again.

Gretchen was back, pressing two fingers to Hayden. "I have a pulse. Let's move."

In a matter of seconds, Hayden was being loaded onto a gurney. My bond mates crowded around her in the back of the ambulance, but I immediately went for shotgun. I couldn't be that close, not knowing that I'd caused this.

Gene hopped behind the wheel and flicked the sirens on again.

"Where's the caster?" Cillian yelled from the back of the ambulance.

"Waiting in medical and preparing everything he'll need," Gene called.

I had a surge of pity for the caster. He was being handed an impossible task, one that when he failed, he'd never be able to stay with our clan. Cillian wouldn't be able to stand the sight of him.

Gene pressed down on the accelerator.

The ride to our territory was made in half the time it normally took. The gates were already open in preparation, and the ambulance didn't even slow as we approached. We screeched to a stop outside our house, members of the horde waiting, wanting to do anything to help.

Knox and Cillian lifted the gurney while Gretchen rode on top of it, squeezing some sort of bag that had to be helping Hayden breathe. I followed behind them as if I were a robot and someone else held my controls.

In some ways, that was exactly true. I'd touched Hayden. Skin-to-skin. I'd felt the mate bond flare to life in my system. She had control now, even if the bond hadn't been cemented.

Cáel and Maddox were practically on top of the gurney as Knox and Cillian guided it down the hall. The moment we reached the medical wing, Marcus, our new caster, was by the gurney's side.

I didn't miss how his face paled as he took in Hayden.

"What happened?" Marcus asked.

All eyes in the room came to me.

"Dragon fire. She got hit with dragon fire." The voice didn't even sound like my own.

Marcus jerked his head in a nod and began grabbing ingredients, mixing them in a bowl. He chanted in that language I still didn't understand as he worked. And a few moments later, he looked up. "I need her mates. All of them."

Panic reared inside me, but a strong hand gripped my arm. I looked down to see Cáel's tattooed hand.

"If you don't help her, I will pull your still-beating heart from your body."

I had no doubt he would. "I'm not going anywhere." I'd do whatever Marcus needed. I had to.

"I need you all to lay hands on her, skin-to-skin," the caster instructed. "Your energy is the only thing that has a prayer of saving her. Picture it flowing into her."

I stepped forward, resting my palm on her calf. Sensation ripped through me, nearly bringing me to my knees. My beast surged to the surface. He wanted free, to claim and protect. He knew his mate was in danger, and he blamed me for it.

I shoved him down, focusing on the feel of Hayden. Her skin was far too cold. It was wrong in every way.

Marcus dipped what looked like a bundle of sage into the concoction he'd created and then held it out to Cillian. "Light it with your fire."

Cillian opened his mouth, and a swirl of flame escaped, lighting the bundle.

"Hands on Hayden," Marcus ordered. "Focus your energy."

I felt that tether between me and Hayden, the one I'd been

trying so desperately to ignore for the last several weeks. Then I shoved everything I had into it. I'd give her the last breath in my lungs if it would help.

Marcus began chanting and sprinkling ash over Hayden's form. The ash wasn't the typical black, though. It was a myriad of colors, changing as it fell.

Suddenly, I felt a tug, a pull on my energy. I let it go, let Hayden take whatever she needed.

That green energy known to casters swirled around Marcus as he chanted louder. Sparks flew around Hayden and then embedded in her chest.

I watched, transfixed as the gaping hole began to heal.

The moment her flesh was knit back together, Marcus slumped against the gurney. He looked at Hayden, no relief in his expression. "All we can do now is wait. It's up to her if she comes back to you."

A different wave of pain hit me at that. Because I'd made Hayden want to run away. I'd made her doubt my bond mates' feelings for her. And if she died now, it would be my fault twice over.

Chapter Three

Hayden

I was flying. All I could feel was the wind on my face and the sensation of being totally and completely weightless. It was heaven.

I dipped, diving toward the ground, then somersaulted before charging upward toward the sky again. A laugh bubbled out of my lips as I rolled to my back, just floating mid-air.

Everything about the sensation was wonderful. I never wanted it to end, yet I could feel a tugging in my chest. Something that was urging me back toward the ground.

I frowned. I didn't want to go down there. I wanted to stay up in the sky, where there were no problems or pain, where I felt free.

"She's frowning. Is she in pain?" a deep voice asked.

That voice was familiar. Some part of me said, *Viking*. But I didn't know what that meant.

"Physically, she's healed. She shouldn't be in pain." The smooth, smoky tone read professor.

"She's been unconscious for a week," the Viking growled, and something smashed.

"You need to shift," the alpha said. "Or your beast is going to do it for you."

"I'm not leaving her."

The pain in the Viking's voice had me lowering myself, dropping slowly toward the ground. I wanted to see him. To comfort him.

It was as if the ground was covered by a thick fog. I had to wade through the haze to find my way toward the voice.

I tried to blink, but my eyelids felt heavy, as if they hadn't lifted in years and had forgotten how to execute the motion. Finally, after several attempts, light flashed across my vision.

"Hayden?" A hand squeezed mine as Knox's warm voice wrapped around me.

He pressed a hand to my cheek. "We're right here. You're okay. You're safe."

Cáel's massive form loomed over me. "Little One?" he croaked.

He looked like heaven and hell all wrapped into one. Just the sight of him eased something in me, but there were dark circles under his bloodshot eyes, and his typically fair skin had a sickly pallor.

"Hi," I rasped.

Cáel dropped his forehead to mine, breathing deeply. "You came back."

His words had memories surging to life. The alley. That awful man. The dragon fire.

I jerked as I remembered the feel of the flames connecting with my chest.

Cáel pulled back but took my hand. "You're safe."

My gaze flew around the room. Knox sat propped next to me in bed, thick scruff along his jaw. Cillian stood, arms crossed, dressed all in black like some dark, avenging angel. Maddox held a clipboard, studying me carefully. And Easton stood on the opposite side of the room, his face an impassive mask.

Cillian prowled toward the bed, his arms dropping to his sides. "How do you feel?"

I tried to take a mental inventory, but my mind was swimming. "Okay, I think. Just tired."

Maddox nodded, adjusting an IV that hung above the bed. "It took a lot of energy for you to heal. You're going to be tired for a while. We've been giving you special vitamins and nutrients intravenously to help you get your strength back."

I studied the bag that hovered above me. It wasn't a typical clear color. It had a greenish hue and seemed to shimmer. *Magic.* I wanted to know everything about how that could be used to help people heal.

Cillian moved to the head of the bed, his hand brushing the hair from my face. "No pain?"

I shook my head. "No."

Remembering the feel of the blast to my chest, I tugged my hands free from Cáel and Knox, careful not to dislodge my IV. My fingers unbuttoned an unfamiliar pajama top so that I could see my chest.

A series of growls filled the air. These weren't ones of possessiveness; these were sounds of anger. The emotion matched the mark on my chest. It looked like a firework of puckered skin. But it also looked far past the healing stage it should've been in.

Cillian pressed a hand over the scar as if he could erase it with his touch. "The injury was severe. There was no way to heal you without scarring."

My gaze lifted to his. "I don't know how it's possible I'm even alive."

Another series of growls swept through the room.

Cáel took my hand again, as if he couldn't stand not touching me. "I'm going to rip Hal apart piece by piece."

A shudder ripped through me at that. "He was a Corbett, wasn't he?"

"Yes," Cillian gritted out. "Their beta. The son of the alpha."

"And he hates you," I surmised.

"From what Easton shared, he hoped to kill Easton and take you," Cillian said, his voice carrying a lethal edge.

My gaze flicked to Easton. He hadn't moved from that spot on the opposite side of the room. He looked the worst of all of them. His eyes had more red in them than any other color. His hair hung in a tangle around his shoulders. It was as if there was no life in him at all.

I stared harder, trying to search for any emotion. Even a flicker of hatred would've been welcome at the moment. But there was nothing.

I bit the inside of my cheek. "Are you okay? You weren't hit?"

Some jolt of energy seemed to zing through Easton's body. His muscles tensed as he pushed off the wall. "Why? Why did you do it?"

Anger vibrated through every word. But I welcomed it. At least his fury meant that Easton wasn't dead after all.

I searched his face, trying to read the root of the anger. My eyes locked with his again, and I didn't look away. "You matter," I said simply. "I know you don't want to matter to me. But you do. It doesn't matter how much of a jerk you are. I wasn't about to let someone kill you."

Easton's chest rose and fell in ragged pants as his back teeth ground together. His lips parted as if he was going to speak, but instead, he turned on his heel and stalked out of the room.

Chapter Four

Hayden

Pain flared in my chest as I watched Easton disappear through the door and down the hallway. Part of me wondered if it was an echo of the injury I'd sustained or if this was just fresh agony from the latest rejection blow.

"I'm so sorry," Knox whispered. His voice was hoarse, layered with his own anguish.

I turned to him, lifting a hand to place over his heart. "It's not your fault."

Knox shook his head. "He's let his fear ruin him, and it almost cost us you. The person we love most. I'll never forgive him for that."

Everything in me twisted. That was the last thing I wanted. The guys needed each other, especially now.

"Don't." I pressed my palm harder against Knox's chest. "He needs you, and you need him just as much."

"I can't, Hayden. He went too far this time."

I kept my hand over Knox's heart but didn't push with words. There'd be time for that. For now, I'd simply assure them all that I was fine.

Something pulsed beneath my palm. Something more than Knox's heartbeat. My brow furrowed as I stared at my hand. It was like I could *feel* Knox. His energy, maybe?

"What?" Knox asked, concern filling his voice.

"Nothing. I just—" I moved my fingers over his pec. "I feel you."

Knox shared a look with the other guys in the room.

Anxiety slid through me. "What? Is something wrong?"

Cillian slid a hand under my tangle of blonde hair. "Easy, Little Flame. You're fine. You're just feeling a deepening of the bond."

I looked up at him in confusion.

"When you were hurt, Easton touched you. He was trying to stop the bleeding."

"Okay..."

"He was the last of your bond mates to have contact. It means that you'll start feeling the pull to us more," Cillian explained.

"It also means that your dragon may surface soon," Maddox added.

"What?" I squeaked.

Knox sent me a gentle smile. "My beast can't wait to meet her."

"Well, tell your beast to chill. I'm not sure I'm ready to transform into a giant lizard."

Knox choked on a laugh.

Cáel frowned down at me. "We're not lizards. We're dragons."

I let out a sound of exasperation. "They look pretty similar to me."

"Not even close," Cillian growled.

"Well, whatever it looks like, I'm not ready."

Maddox studied me for a moment. "Your animal half needs to spread her wings at some point. She's been pushed down for so long that if you keep her locked away, she may fight you for dominance."

A shiver ran through me. "Like she won't let me turn back into a human?"

"Yes," he answered matter-of-factly.

Panic flared hot and fast, and my gaze jerked around the room as if my dragon were about to jump out and take me hostage.

Cillian squeezed the back of my neck again. "Breathe, Little Flame. I'll help you."

"How?" I demanded.

"He's the alpha," Knox explained. "Your dragon will recognize his authority."

"Unless she goes feral," Cáel muttered.

"Feral?" I squeaked.

"Not helping," Cillian growled. He turned to me. "An animal going feral is extremely rare. We're going to welcome your dragon when she comes out, make her feel safe and cherished. The fact that she'll have her mates around her will help."

My head swirled as I lay back on the pillows. "This is a lot to take in."

The room went quiet. *Too* quiet.

I glared at them all. "What else is there?"

My focus shifted to Maddox, whose mouth had pressed into a hard line. "Tell me."

He would say whatever it was scientifically. Straight facts.

Maddox shifted uncomfortably. "Now that all of us have touched you, there's something else to consider."

"What?" I demanded.

"Just like the presence and touch of your mates can bring about your shift, it can also bring your heat."

I blinked a few times. "Heat? Like my ability to breathe fire?"

The panic was back. What if I hurt someone?

"No," Knox assured me. "That comes with the shift."

"Great," I muttered. "So, what the hell is my heat?"

Everyone was quiet.

"Someone start talking!" I yelled.

"It means your time of being fertile," Maddox finally said.

"I'm sorry, did you say *fertile*? Like I could get knocked up with a bunch of dragon babies?"

Maddox winced. "Yes. It means that you could get pregnant. But it, um, also means that, uh—"

"Spit it out already," I demanded.

Cillian squeezed the back of my neck again. "You'll have touch hunger. You'll need sexual contact often and for great lengths of time. It will be painful and can reach points of agony if you don't have it."

My jaw went completely slack.

Not only was I going to turn into a giant, flying lizard, but I was also going to turn into a sex maniac. Awesome.

Knox stroked a hand over my cheek. "We'll get you through it. It might be scary the first time, but we'll all be there."

Maddox cleared his throat. "I'm going to get Hayden something to eat. We'll start with soup."

He was gone before anyone could respond.

Cáel glared after him.

So not everyone would be there. Not Maddox. And certainly not Easton.

Cillian bent, his lips ghosting over my temple. "It's going to be okay."

Pressure built behind my eyes. The urge to cry was so strong, but I knew if I let the dam break now, the tears would never stop. So, I forced them down, something I was becoming far too good at. But I'd have to get even better.

Because even though I was tied to five men, only three of them wanted me. And I wasn't sure if that was because of who I was or because of the damn bond.

Chapter Five

Hayden

"You're sure you feel up to going back to class?" Knox asked for the twelfth time this morning.

I fought the urge to throw something at him. "I stayed in bed for four days and took it easy for another three. I'm starting to go stir-crazy."

Cáel pulled me into him, but the action was gentle, as if I were made from the most delicate glass. "You should take at least another two weeks."

I pinched his side lightly. "I'm fine."

And I was starting to lose it with the way the guys were hovering. Maddox and Easton kept their distance, but there was still that air. Even now, Easton stood by the front door, simply waiting, not saying a word.

There was tension between him and the rest of his brothers. Tension that had guilt gnawing at me. Yes, it was Easton's cruel words that had sent me running. But I was the idiot who'd run out of the club without protection. But every time I tried to talk to Easton, he dodged me.

I never thought that I'd prefer Easton's snide comments and rude remarks, but they were a hell of a lot better than this careful silence. Everything about the way things were was too quiet. There was no laughter or life. The guys didn't tease and play. And they sure as hell weren't touching me.

My mouth pulled into a scowl as I bent to pick up my backpack. But Cáel snatched it up before I could lift it. I glared at him, extending my hand.

"I've got it."

I narrowed my eyes, not moving my hand.

Cáel averted his eyes.

"You shouldn't be lifting heavy things," Knox said softly.

I turned to face him. "Marcus said I'm 100 percent healed."

Knox wasn't so easily cowed by my angry stare. "He also said that you need to take it easy for another week."

"As in, I shouldn't start training for a marathon, not that I can't carry my own bag."

"Let them take care of you, Little Flame. They need it," Cillian said, striding through the entryway, looking devastating in his black suit.

My glare shifted to him.

Cillian just laughed and gently tugged me into his arms. His lips brushed over my temple. "I'm glad to see you're feeling better."

I grumbled something not all that warm and welcoming under my breath. But my body was a complete traitor. It came alive under the briefest touch. It was as if my nerve endings stood and stretched, reaching for more of Cillian. Only I knew I'd never get it.

Just as quickly as he'd pulled me into his hold, Cillian released me. "You guys better get going, or you'll be late."

I gnashed my back teeth together, swallowing down a snippy retort. I knew that the guys had been through their own ordeal. I'd scared the hell out of them when I'd been hit with that dragon fire.

But I was starting to feel like some sort of jewel they wanted to hide away instead of their mate.

"Hayden," Cillian called as I started toward the door.

I turned to look at him, but I couldn't force out any words.

His gaze swept over me, and I swore I saw a hint of fear in his expression for the briefest second.

"We'll have two enforcers patrolling campus, and Knox, Cáel, and Easton will meet you between classes. You go nowhere alone. Promise me."

It wasn't a question. It was a demand. But I didn't have it in me to challenge him.

"I promise."

There was no life in my voice, no spark. I was too tired.

We filed out of the house and climbed into Easton's G-Wagon. I was quiet on the ride to campus, simply staring out the window, watching the forests and town pass. I felt a pang when we passed Spark's Diner. Cillian had already informed Fiona that I wouldn't be working there any longer. It was too risky.

Hal Corbett had gone into hiding, but that didn't mean that other Corbett clan members weren't waiting to pounce. From the little I'd managed to overhear, tensions were running high between the two hordes. One wrong move and there would be an all-out war.

"You remember the cover story?" Knox asked from up front where he was riding shotgun.

I swallowed hard, not moving my gaze from the window as Easton parked. "I was getting some air in the alley at Ashes & Emeralds, and someone tried to mug me. They heard Easton coming, got spooked, and shot me. I didn't see their face."

The cop that had finally been allowed to question me hadn't seemed all that concerned about my so-called attack. He told me to stay away from dangerous clubs and left. But I guessed with no ID or bullet, what was he supposed to do?

Cáel reached over and squeezed my thigh. "You don't have to do this."

I watched as students strode into the various academic buildings. This was exactly what I needed. School had always been my one grounding force. I'd need it now more than ever. So, I opened my door and slid out.

Cáel had been right. I should've stayed home.

"I heard she was giving someone a blow job in the alley, and then he just shot her when she was done," one girl whispered to another as I headed down the hallway.

My shoulders slumped. The rumor mill had apparently been flying in the week since I'd been out of classes, and I was sure I had Delaney to thank for a large portion of it. I hated to admit it, but I was exhausted. My muscles ached, and my brain was foggy. All I wanted was a long nap.

I rounded the corner of the science building, knowing that one of the two enforcers on Hayden duty would be trailing behind. They had been all day long.

"Hayden," an annoyed voice clipped.

My head jerked up to find Professor Brent glowering at me.

The pressure built behind my eyes. The last thing I needed to deal with after the longest day known to man was him.

"Professor," I greeted.

"My office. *Now.*"

Shit. Shit. Shit.

I glanced behind me at my shadow, Pete. His usually easygoing expression was tight, but there was nothing he could do without exposing himself.

"Now," Brent pushed.

I sighed and followed him down the hall to his small office. The space was crammed with books but still managed to fit a desk, two chairs for students, and a leather couch.

"Sit," Brent ordered, gesturing to the couch.

I bit the inside of my cheek but did as he commanded.

"I have sent you half a dozen emails. I had to hear from the dean that you were *shot*. What the hell is going on?"

I laced my hands in my lap as my advisor lowered himself to the couch next to me. "I'm sorry. I still haven't gotten to my emails. I've been recovering and trying to catch up on the schoolwork I've missed."

The truth was, I was now ahead in all my classes. I'd been bored as hell this past week and read ahead in just about every subject.

Brent's mouth pressed into a firm line. "I'm glad to hear that you're staying focused on your studies, but that doesn't mean you haven't put your academic career at great risk. What the hell were you thinking going to a club like that alone?"

I blinked up at him. "I wasn't alone."

My advisor's expression went thunderous. "Who were you with?"

I swallowed hard, choosing my words carefully. "My boyfriend."

Redness crept up Brent's throat. "And that would be?"

"Knox Gallagher."

The redness intensified as Brent's jaw worked back and forth. "Mr. Gallagher and his *roommates* are bad news. I thought you were taking your academic career seriously. That you wanted to be a doctor."

"I do. I am. I've submitted all my missed assignments and rescheduled any tests and quizzes I need to make up."

The professor's expression softened, and he dropped a hand to my leg. He made it seem like he was aiming for my knee, but it was too high for that. My stomach roiled and pitched as he squeezed my leg.

"I'm glad to hear it, Hayden. We'll just have to stick together to make sure you achieve those dreams."

Chapter Six

Cael

I followed Hayden's scent down the hallway of the science building. It was faint now, mixed with the smells of humans, but just that hint of her was enough to take the edge off my beast. He'd been riding me all day. Since I didn't have any classes with Hayden, I hadn't seen her much, and my animal wasn't pleased.

Ever since we'd all touched her, the need to be close to Hayden had intensified. Add to that the fact that we'd almost lost her, and it was a miracle my dragon hadn't gone feral yet.

Just the memory of it had scales rippling across my back. I struggled to bring my ragged breathing under control.

Knox fell into step beside me. "You okay?"

I jerked my head in a nod, not able to speak just yet.

"You ready to head home?"

I nodded again. "Where's East?"

My voice was rougher than normal, a telltale sign my beast was close to the surface.

Knox surveyed me again, and I didn't miss the concern in his eyes.

"East?" I pressed, desperate to get the focus off me.

Knox turned back to the hallway ahead, now mostly empty of students. "Dunno. At the car, probably."

My steps faltered. Knox always knew where his twin was. But since the incident, he'd barely been able to look at Easton, let alone talk to him. The new normal had me twitchy, the feeling of our unbalanced bond settling in deep.

I clenched and flexed my hands at my sides. "Do you…uh… want to talk about it?"

I wasn't good at this crap. Talking. Feelings. I'd shut all of that off for so long that it seemed impossible to open it up again. With anyone but Hayden.

Knox's gaze flicked to me. At first, his expression was full of annoyance, but it quickly melted away. His shoulders slumped as he sighed. "I've dealt with his bullshit for years. I understand it. But he went too far this time. I could kill him for putting Hayden at risk, but more than that, he's made her doubt us."

I stopped dead in my tracks at that. "What do you mean?"

Knox slowed, turning to face me. "Haven't you felt it? She's hesitant with us now. Unsure. She doesn't know if we want *her* or if this is just the bond controlling us all."

"It's both." The words were out of my mouth before I could stop them. I shook my head. "We're a bond because we balance each other. Because…" I struggled to find the right words.

"I know," Knox assured me. "We're perfect complements. There's no way we couldn't be drawn to one another, but that just means we appreciate all the unique intricacies of Hayden like no one else would."

I grunted. Knox was always better with words than I was. But maybe that was okay. Because I brought other things to the table.

Footsteps sounded in the hallway, and I turned to see Easton striding toward us. He frowned. "Where's Hayden?"

Knox scowled at his twin, not saying a word.

"We were just going to find her. She's got Pete with her," I hurried to explain.

Knox started walking again, eager to avoid his brother. I didn't miss the slight stoop to Easton's shoulders at Knox's rejection. Hell, those two needed to work this out in the fight circle.

I moved after Knox, coming up short as we rounded the corner and found Pete standing alone in the hallway. Everything in me tensed. "Where's Hayden?"

Pete scowled. "With her advisor. I couldn't exactly follow her inside."

Easton tensed at my side. "Brent?"

Pete nodded.

Easton muttered a curse.

"What?" I demanded.

Easton's jaw clenched. "I don't like the way he treats her. I get a bad vibe."

Without waiting for anything from us, Easton strode up to the door and knocked. Loudly.

"Come in," an annoyed voice said.

I stepped to the side so I could get a slice of a view of the room. Hayden was hurrying to her feet and grabbing her bag. Her face was paler than I'd seen it since her attack.

A growl built in my throat, and Knox grabbed me by the shirt.

"Keep it together," he bit out.

"She's upset," I said through gritted teeth.

"I. Know."

"Hello, Professor," Easton said with a fake smile. "I had a question about the group project for psych."

The professor glared up at East. "These aren't my office hours. You can ask me in class tomorrow."

Hayden rounded the teacher, giving him a wide berth as she slid out of his office. "Thanks for your help, Professor," she muttered.

"We're not done, Ms. Parrish," Brent clipped.

Knox stepped forward then. "Hi, baby." He wrapped an arm

around her shoulders and gave the professor an easy wave. "Doctor said Hayden needs her rest, so she's gotta get home."

Professor Brent snapped his mouth closed, but his gaze focused in on the arm around Hayden's shoulders.

Another growl built in my chest, but I swallowed it down.

"We'll see you in class tomorrow," Easton said, forcing the teacher's attention back to him.

He muttered something under his breath as he shut the door in Easton's face.

Knox was already guiding Hayden down the hallway, away from the male none of us liked.

Easton fell into step next to me. "I don't have a good feeling about him."

Neither did I.

Chapter Seven

Hayden

"What happened in there?" Knox asked softly.

I knew he could feel my body trembling against his. But I didn't want to lay this at his feet. The guys were already worried enough about me. If they knew my professor was being a total creeper, they'd lose it.

"He got on me for missing school. I hate feeling like I'm in trouble."

It wasn't a lie. All of those things were true. I just left out the part about his hand on my leg. But I'd dealt with that. I'd moved, scrunching my body against the arm of the couch.

An image filled my mind of Professor Brent's face. The way it had twisted in anger just before Easton had knocked on the door.

"He thinks you were fucking shot, and he's giving you shit about missing a few classes?" Easton clipped. "I know you already turned in all your assignments."

My gaze flicked to him. How did Easton know about my studies?

"He knows I want to go to medical school and that I'll need a scholarship. I have to have impeccable grades for that."

Knox glanced down at me. "You don't need a scholarship."

I halted in the middle of the empty hallway. "Uh, yeah. I do." It wasn't like I was a secret billionaire.

Knox grinned. "If you haven't noticed, we're kind of rolling in it."

"Yeah. *You* are. Not me."

Knox's amusement quickly transformed into a scowl. "Whatever is ours is yours. That's the way it works."

My heart beat faster. "No, it's not. It's yours. I'm not just going to take your money. It's bad enough that you won't let me pay rent. I'd never just let you cover sixty grand a year for my school."

I slid out of Knox's hold and kept walking. I needed Cillian to deal with the Corbetts however he was going to so that I could get back to my job at the diner. I needed that sense of self-sufficiency, of control.

Knox hurried to catch up to me, Cáel, Easton, and Pete trailing behind. "You want to work yourself to the bone instead of just letting us help you?"

"Yes," I snapped.

He caught my arm, stopping me. "Why?"

"Because I take care of myself. You don't have to fix everything."

Hurt flashed across Knox's face, and I instantly wanted to take back my words.

A burn lit in my eyes. "I'm sorry," I whispered. I sent up a million silent curses as tears filled my eyes. "I'm used to taking care of myself. Everything is changing, and I just need some of that normalcy."

Knox wrapped his arms around me, pulling me into his chest. "I'm sorry. I was pushy. I know this is new. But it's in our nature to want to take care of you, to tend to all your needs. I know how easy it would be for us to pay for your education, so it seems silly not to. But if you want to get a scholarship, then I'll be your best study buddy for the next four years."

A tiny laugh escaped me, muffled by Knox's chest. "Thank you. I'd much rather have a study buddy than a blank check."

Knox dropped a kiss to the top of my head. "Understood."

I felt heat at my back and twisted in Knox's hold to find the source.

Cáel hovered close, his face twisted in worry. "You're okay?"

Guilt swamped me, and I sniffed. "I'm okay, Big Guy."

He didn't look convinced.

I pushed out of Knox's hold and wrapped my arms around Cáel's waist. "I promise. This has all just been…a lot."

Cáel pulled back a fraction to take in my face. "You mean it's not every day you find out you're going to transform into an overgrown lizard and have five mates for all eternity?"

I choked on a laugh. "Cáel, you've got jokes."

He grinned and shrugged.

"If it isn't the little faker," a voice singsonged from down the hallway.

Delaney made her way toward us, with Maggie and Bella in tow. "What lengths won't she go to for attention?"

Maggie and Bella shared a nervous look but didn't say a word.

"Shove a sock in it, Delaney," Easton muttered. "Nobody needs your nasty-ass bullshit today."

She huffed as she flicked her dark locks over her shoulder. "What? Now I'm not allowed to state an opinion? I might hurt your whore's feelings?"

Cáel let out a growl that had Delaney stumbling back a few steps and straight into Maggie and Bella.

"Ow," Maggie squealed. "Watch it."

Delaney turned her glare on Maggie. "Shut up."

Maggie's cheeks went pink, and she opened her mouth as if she might tell Delaney off, but whatever she saw in her queen bee's eyes made her snap her mouth closed.

Delaney turned back to us, her gaze settling on me. "People are going to find out the truth about you. I hope you're ready for that, slut."

I was tired. So damned tired it felt like my bones ached. There was a part of me that just wanted to lie down and take Delaney's bullshit. But I'd dealt with the crude comments one too many times today.

I shrugged out of Cáel's hold and took a step toward her. I smiled as angelically as I could. "Delaney, it's so sweet of you to be so concerned for me. I was so lucky to have you as my roommate for those first few weeks. But I promise, you don't have to look out for me anymore." I leaned forward, picking up a stage whisper. "People might start to think you're a little obsessed with me. We wouldn't want that."

Easton choked on a laugh behind me, while Knox started coughing. Cáel simply grunted.

Delaney's face turned the shade of a tomato. "I am not obsessed with you."

I gave her a look of mock confusion. "You're not? I don't know, you sure talk about me a lot. Try to find out details about my life, who I spend time with, and what I'm doing. I can see how people might misconstrue that."

Bella rolled her lips over her teeth in an attempt to keep in her laughter as Delaney sputtered.

"I just think people should know the truth about who's in their midst," Delaney argued.

"Oh?" I asked innocently. "And who's that? Someone who is perfectly happy minding her own business and not bothering anyone?"

"You said you were sleeping with Knox *and* Cáel!"

I shrugged. "So? Why do you care?" I made an over-exaggerated pause. "Could it be because you've been working on some sort of warped plan to get Knox to yourself? Or was that Cillian?

They're honestly interchangeable to you because you don't know either of them."

Knox scoffed behind me. "Wouldn't touch her with a ten-foot pole."

"Guess you'll need to be focused on Cillian, then. Good luck with that," I said nonchalantly as I started walking again. I was so beyond done with this day.

Delaney spat curses after me, but I didn't let any of them land. I just kept right on walking.

Knox jogged to catch up with me, slinging an arm over my shoulders. "That was a thing of beauty."

I shook my head. "Can we go home now?"

It was Easton who answered as he, Cáel, and Pete reached us. "Please, before Cáel guts Delaney in the hallway."

Cáel grunted. "She's a woman. I'd make it more painless. I'd just snap her neck."

I couldn't help it; I laughed and patted his chest. "Such a gentleman."

Knox's phone rang, and he pulled it out of his pocket. He grinned as he put it on speaker. "Cill, you would not believe the verbal bitch-slap our girl just laid down."

"Not now, Knox," Cillian clipped.

Everyone stilled.

"We have a major problem. The dragon council is here."

Chapter Eight

Hayden

THE CURSES AND GROWLS THAT FILLED THE AIR TOLD me the dragon council wasn't anything good, but I still had about a million questions.

"Where is *here*?" Easton gritted out.

"The house," Cillian answered, tension running through his words.

"Right now?" Knox demanded.

"Showed up unannounced. It's not like I had a choice whether to let them in," Cillian muttered.

Cáel moved in closer, surrounding me with his massive body.

"What's the play?" Easton asked.

Cillian let out an audible breath across the line. "We don't have much room to maneuver. They're demanding to see Hayden."

"No," Cáel spat, making me jump.

"We have to," Cillian said calmly.

My gaze ping-ponged between all the men in the hallway, trying to figure out what the hell was going on.

Knox glared down at his phone. "How the hell did they find out about her?"

"Corbetts," Easton muttered. "Had to be."

"That's my guess, as well," Cillian agreed. "Probably trying to cover their asses after almost killing Hayden."

Cáel growled low, making the hairs on my arm stand on end.

"Like we'd ever take our problems to the council," Knox spat.

"Well, they weren't taking any chances. I told Maddox to meet you at Easton's car. Prepare Hayden the best you can on the ride home," Cillian ordered.

Knox glanced at Easton and Cáel. "Are you sure that's a good idea?"

"Which part?"

"All of it, but I was thinking about involving Mad," Knox answered.

Cillian sighed. "It would be worse if he found out about their presence later."

Easton muttered something under his breath.

"Make it quick," Cillian ordered. "It'll just get worse the longer they have to wait."

He hung up without another word.

Everyone was quiet for a moment before I spoke. "What the hell is the dragon council?"

"We'll explain in the car," Knox said. "We need to move."

Pete was already on his phone, talking to his enforcer partner, Terry. Cáel kept an arm around me as he hurried me down the hallway and out into the late afternoon sunshine. We crossed the parking lot to find Maddox standing at the G-Wagon.

I'd never seen him quite as he was right now. A fury radiated through Maddox, practically vibrating his body as he waited for our approach.

Easton approached him warily. "You going to be okay?"

"Yes." Maddox's voice sounded more animal than human, and I knew for certain he was anything but okay.

Pete and Terry got into the SUV next to ours as Maddox and Easton got into the front seats of ours. Cáel opened the door for me, and I slid into the center back seat. With Knox and Cáel on either side of me, I had to twist my body sideways to fit.

"Start talking," I ordered as Easton backed out of the parking spot.

Knox and Easton shared a look through the rearview mirror. It felt like some silent twin-speak passed between them before Knox began to talk.

"For a long time, we had a ruling class. A queen and her bond who oversaw all the hordes across the globe. Each individual horde had its own ruling figures. Some were called kings and queens, an honor passed through bloodlines. Others had alphas, who were chosen through dominance."

"You have an alpha. Cillian is the most dominant dragon?" I asked.

Knox nodded. "That's how our horde was formed. We really didn't give Cillian much of a choice."

"And no one just votes? Like a dragon democracy?" I asked.

Knox's lips twitched. "I don't think that's really a thing."

"It should be," I mumbled.

He linked his fingers through mine. "Over the years, there were more and more attempts on the queen's life. More and more infighting. There were forces calling for change. That we should have a council that represented all the quadrants of the globe."

"That sounds fair."

Cáel grunted next to me.

"It's honestly just people grasping for more power," Knox explained. "From the stories my parents told me, the queen and her bond really cared for our people. Who we have now seems to be more concerned with control and prestige."

"What happened to the queen?" I asked.

A shadow passed over Knox's eyes. "She and her bond were killed in an attack. The new council stepped in days later."

I gaped at him. "You think they had her killed."

"That's what most believe," Easton said.

My gaze flicked to the front seats. Maddox's hands were clenched so tightly that his knuckles had no color in them at all, while Easton simply looked sad.

"And they're here? Why?" I asked Knox.

He sent a worried look around the vehicle. "They want to know whenever a female dragon is born or discovered."

A heavy weight settled in my stomach. "Why?"

Knox gripped my hand tighter. "I said they like control. They see female dragons as pawns, ways to access more power."

That weight only intensified. "But they're people."

"I know. But there are hordes all over the world who would give *anything* for a dragon mate."

Panic zipped through me, blood roaring in my ears. "But I have my mates."

Easton's gaze found mine in the mirror. "You could choose to leave us if you wanted."

"But they can't make me, right?" My anxiety radiated in each of my words.

"They won't take you," Cáel growled, moving in impossibly closer.

Knox's gaze locked with mine. "But they will manipulate you with everything they have to get you to make that choice."

Chapter Nine

Hayden

The moment the words were out of Knox's mouth, Cáel unbuckled my seat belt and hauled me onto his lap. "No."

His arms wrapped tightly around me as if I might disappear.

Knox and Easton shared a look through the rearview mirror. Maddox still stared straight ahead, unmoving.

I nuzzled into Cáel. The scent of snow and that hint of smoke swirled around me. I could feel his heartbeat, pounding in a rapid rhythm against my body. I pressed my palm to his chest. "I'm right here. I'm not going anywhere."

I said it for myself as much as for Cáel. But my stomach churned as if I'd taken to rough seas.

Knox sent me a reassuring smile, but it was strained at the edges. "We won't leave you alone with them. I promise."

I let out a shuddering breath. That helped. As strained as things had been lately, I knew that these guys would always have my back against a threat.

Easton glanced at me through the rearview mirror. I couldn't read his expression. The mixture of emotions flitted across his face too quickly for me to pin down a single one.

He slowed at the gate, rolled down his window, and pressed a hand to the palm reader. The gates opened, and my stomach cramped.

I pressed my face to Cáel's neck and breathed deeply. His scent stilled a restless energy inside me, a fluttering. And Cáel let out a rumbling growl that sounded more like a purr.

As Easton navigated the gravel roads toward the house, Cáel's arms tightened around me. By the time Easton pulled to a stop, I could barely breathe.

None of us moved for a moment, just staring at the house and the unfamiliar SUV parked in front of us.

Finally, Knox spoke. "We're just going to make it worse by waiting."

Cáel grunted but opened the door. He didn't, however, let me go. He slid us out of the vehicle and hauled me into his arms, cradling me against his chest.

"Put her down, man," Easton warned.

"No."

Cáel was back to single words and grunts. Maybe it was more of his animal side taking over, trying to protect him.

I pressed a kiss to the hollow of his throat, to the swirl of ink there. "I'll be okay. You'll be right there with me."

"It'll go better if she walks in on her own two feet," Knox said.

My gaze found Maddox. He stood nearby, but he might as well have been a million miles away. There was a glassy, unfocused quality to his amber eyes that set me on edge.

Cáel's hold on me loosened slightly, and he dropped my feet to the ground. "Stay close."

I looked up at him. "Always."

His head lowered, and he took my mouth. For the first time since the attack, Cáel kissed me. *Really* kissed me. This was no polite and gentle lip touch. This was *Cáel*. He plundered my mouth, his tongue demanding entrance.

My body answered instantly, pressing up against his and tipping my head back to grant him better access. Cáel's tongue teased and stroked, sending waves of need coursing through me.

A throat cleared, and I jerked back.

Easton inclined his head toward the house. "We need to go."

Knox shook his head. "Thanks for making me meet the dragon council with a hard-on. That'll be fun."

My cheeks flushed, and I ducked my head.

Cáel scowled at him. "Don't embarrass her."

"Embarrass *her*?" Knox protested. "I'm the one going in there hard as a fucking rock. I look like I'm going through puberty a second time."

I glanced at Maddox. He still had no reaction. Dread pooled in my belly, and I moved in his direction. "Are you okay?" I whispered.

He blinked a few times as if just realizing I was there. "Fine," he clipped and headed for the front door.

That went well.

Knox squeezed my shoulder as he pitched his voice low. "Don't take it personally. Mad has bad blood with the council."

I looked up at him, a million questions in my gaze. But I knew none of them would be answered.

Maddox opened the door and strode inside. We followed behind. The moment we were in the entryway, Knox took one side of me, Cáel the other. They boxed me in, so it was hard to even move.

Easton and Maddox led the way toward a formal living room I'd never spent any time in. Unfamiliar voices filtered through the air, and a wave of nausea swept through me.

"Ah, here they are," a feminine voice crooned.

"Late," a male voice chastised.

"It would've had to have been a *planned* visit for them to be late, Nolan." Cillian's voice sounded as if he were reprimanding a child.

The other man grumbled something under his breath.

As Maddox and Easton parted, I could finally take in the room. Four strangers were perched on various pieces of furniture. As different as they all looked, they had one thing in common. They were stunningly beautiful.

The sole female looked to be in her late twenties. She sat on a tufted chair, in a pose that would've been fit for an oil painting. She wore leather pants that fit her like a glove, paired with stiletto heels and a blouse that I'd be far too terrified of spilling something on to ever wear.

Her hair was a vibrant red and spilled around her shoulders in perfect curls. The only thing that overshadowed the tendrils were her piercing green eyes. Eyes that were locked on me. Assessing.

I winced as I thought about what I was wearing. I at least had on one of the new pairs of jeans the guys had gifted me and new Vans. But my T-shirt was an old one of mine that read, *Never Trust an Atom, They Make Up Everything*. Not exactly my best first impression.

A man with dark skin and wearing a perfectly tailored suit reclined on the couch. He took a sip of an amber liquid as he studied me. "Interesting."

"Fionn," the woman chided, amusement in her voice.

A second man scowled in my direction. He wore khakis and a preppy sweater. The combination of that with his blond hair and blue eyes made him seem like he'd be more at home at a yacht club. "This is highly inappropriate," he chastised. "You should've called us immediately."

Cillian lounged on the couch looking entirely unruffled. "There's no law stating we need to inform you that we've found our mate, Arthur."

Movement caught my attention as a fourth man shoved off the bar and stalked forward. He, too, wore a suit. He had silver threaded through his dark hair, and his tanned skin held lines around his eyes. But something told me those lines weren't from smiling.

"He's right, Cillian." The man's voice sent a chill skating down my spine. "The council must be informed when a new dragon is found." He flashed me a smile. Everything about it was fake, from the too-white teeth to the strained muscles in his cheeks. "After all, we can't have Hayden being brainwashed before she's had a chance to choose her future for herself."

Maddox let out a low growl.

The man's smile only grew. "Careful, Maddox. I might see that as a sign of aggression."

Cillian wrapped his hand around a crystal glass. "I think it's you who might need to be careful, Nolan. It sounded like you were insulting me and my family."

There was a flicker of *something* in Nolan's expression. Anger? Fear? I wasn't entirely sure.

Nolan waved Cillian off. "Nothing of the sort. But it is my responsibility to let Hayden know she has choices. My responsibility is to introduce her to other hordes who are looking for a mate. You don't have a problem with that, do you?"

Chapter Ten

Cillian

My dragon pushed against my skin, surging to the surface and desperately trying to break free. He wanted to annihilate the man who stood in our living room, threatening to take our mate. He wanted to unsheathe his claws and spill Nolan's intestines out onto the rug.

I forced my beast down.

We had to play this smart. Nolan certainly was. He knew that if he got under our skin and one of us snapped, he'd have cause to remove Hayden from our care. I wasn't about to give him that.

I pushed to my feet, crossing in front of Nolan and straight to Hayden. Knox stepped back, giving me space. My hand slipped beneath her gorgeous blonde tendrils, and I squeezed her neck.

It was a possessive hold. Every dragon in the room would recognize it as such. Everyone except Hayden.

She tipped her head back, looking up at me with such sweet submission. But there was fear and uncertainty in those hypnotizing violet eyes. The fact that Nolan had put those emotions there had me wanting to gut him all over again.

I dipped my head, brushing my lips across Hayden's. It was a blatant *fuck you* to the council, but I didn't give a damn.

Hayden melted into me, and I had to fight the urge to throw her over my shoulder and run fast and far. Everything in me wanted to create distance from the threat all around us.

I forced myself to pull away from Hayden's mouth, her taste, and her jasmine and fresh dew scent. I knew my eyes had likely gone dark, but it couldn't be helped. "Hayden is free to meet whomever she would like. And she's also free to opt out of those meetings."

Nolan's brown eyes swirled gold. "You don't have a say in that."

"*Boys*," Mona warned, uncrossing and recrossing her legs. "Let's not allow this conversation to devolve."

Nolan flicked her a look of annoyance, and as much as Mona pissed me off at times, I wanted to buy her a bottle of the god-awful vodka she favored. His focus returned to me. "Cillian needs to be reminded of his *place*. He already executed an alpha, a *king* of one of the hordes, without council authorization."

My body went rigid as fury blazed through me. My beast pulled at the reins, dying to break free. "I killed my *father* when he attempted to slay my little brother. When he almost succeeded."

I could still see the blast of alpha fire hit Declan in the chest, see his body fall, his mate weeping over him. I wished I could've killed Patrick over and over again. But even if I could do it every day for the rest of my life, it wouldn't satiate my anger.

Hayden's hand fisted in my button-down, her muscles tensing as she looked up at me in question.

Nolan picked up on it instantly. He grinned at her. "Your so-called mate didn't tell you that he murdered his father?"

Maddox let out another growl. "You're the only ones who let people get away with murder around here."

Oh, hell. I could hear the fury in Mad's voice. He was seconds away from snapping.

I sent Easton a sharp look.

He quickly stepped up next to Maddox, so close that he could grab him if Mad were to truly snap. "Are you here to investigate Hal Corbett's attack on Hayden?"

I had to give it to Easton. His question sounded so innocent, as if he believed the council would actually work against injustice. But we knew the truth. Their fancy clothes, expensive cars, and palatial homes were bought with bribes from hordes all over the world.

Nolan's eyes flashed. "Hal did report an incident to us. One that we were extremely concerned about."

Fionn set his glass of scotch down on the side table. "He said that you attacked him, Easton. That a female dragon got caught in the crossfire."

Hayden surged forward before I could stop her. "That's not true. Easton didn't do anything. That monster attacked us."

Pain streaked across Easton's face. Agony at the memory and that she was still trying to protect him, even though he didn't deserve it.

Interest flickered in Mona's eyes. "I know it can be hard, being introduced to a whole new world. You don't always understand the dynamics of the supernatural world."

Hayden glared at her. "I know when someone shoots a fireball at us out of nowhere. I'm not an idiot."

Our girl had fire. And I loved her for it. But in this situation, that fire could get us into a hell of a lot of hot water.

Arthur scoffed as he ran his hand through his perfectly coiffed hair. "You know nothing about our world, girl."

Redness crept up Hayden's throat. "I know that I'm happy here and that I don't want to meet any other hordes or whatever else you had in mind. Just leave me alone."

Nolan's eyes narrowed. "Careful. I might take that as an insult."

Cáel moved then, hauling Hayden back against his chest. "Back off."

"You don't get to make that call," Nolan spat back. "Unless you're challenging our authority?"

"No one is doing that," I interjected. "But Hayden does still have free will, *doesn't she*?"

A mixture of anger and agony bled into those words as I locked eyes with Nolan. He knew exactly what I meant. He was the one member of the council who had been in leadership all those years ago when I'd tried to file my report. When I'd told them of the atrocities my so-called father had committed. When I still believed the council did some good.

But Nolan hadn't given one flying fuck. Because he'd been in my father's pocket all along.

Mona stood, feeling the building tension. "Of course, she does. But a girl's gotta know her options so she can make an *informed* decision. So, we've planned a little cocktail party for the weekend. All eligible and appropriate hordes have been invited. Then Hayden can make her own choice."

But I knew what that meant. All hordes that had paid the council to be invited. Hordes that would do anything for a mate. Even if that meant taking her.

Chapter Eleven

Hayden

"ARE YOU SURE YOU DON'T WANT SOMETHING TO eat?" Knox asked for the sixth time.

I shook my head. "I'm not hungry."

Cáel frowned. "You need to eat. It's how you heal."

I sighed. "It's been a day, guys. I'll eat a good breakfast tomorrow."

How the hell was I supposed to have an appetite when bomb after bomb had been dropped, and it was clear there were a million secrets still being kept? It was clear as day that both Maddox and Cillian had a river of bad blood with the council. But both had disappeared the moment the council members had left. Easton had been close on their heels.

Knox and Cáel had stuck close, but I was honestly starting to feel a little suffocated. I pushed up off the couch.

They both started to rise, but I held out a hand to stop them. "Thank you. For being here. For supporting me. You both mean more to me than you'll ever know." Those three little words were on the tip of my tongue, but I swallowed them back. "I just need some time to process, okay?"

Cáel frowned. "Alone?"

Damn it. This felt like kicking a puppy.

I crossed to him, stepping between his legs. I ran my hand over his head, his silky blond braids and dreads sifting through my fingers. Leaning down, I took his mouth. The kiss wasn't aggressive; it was comfort and reassurance. I poured everything into it that I couldn't give voice to yet.

When I pulled back, Cáel's eyes were hooded. I traced my fingers over the tattoos on his neck. "Always with you."

A tenderness filled his expression that had a burn lighting my throat. He pressed a fist to his chest. "Always in here."

"Always," I whispered.

I released my hold on Cáel and moved to Knox. He sent me a hesitant smile. "We're hovering again, aren't we?"

My lips twitched. "Maybe just a little."

Knox pulled me toward him, his hands on my ass. "We hover because we care."

My hands rested on his shoulders. "I know. It's been a really long time since anyone has had my back. I'm still just getting used to it."

Knox scowled. "I wish we'd been there for you from the beginning."

I bent, kissing him deeply, warmth spreading through me at the contact. "You're here now."

Straightening, I stepped out of his hold. "I'll be back."

Cáel full-on pouted, but Knox smacked him with a pillow. "Come on. Let's play some Xbox."

Cáel grunted but picked up a controller. They'd be okay.

I made my way out of the family room and down the hallway. I hadn't lied. I did need some time to process. But that processing required answers. And Cillian was the one who'd have them.

I tried his office first, thinking he might have holed up there, but the space was dark. I opted for his bedroom next, but that, too, was empty. I stood in the hallway, thinking. Then I remembered another room.

Following the maze that was this house, I finally found the door that led to the basement. As I opened it, faint strains of hard-hitting rock reached my ears. Bingo.

I headed down the stairs, stopping short in the massive, state-of-the-art gym. It had more machines and equipment than I could quickly count. But my eyes zeroed in on one thing.

Cillian.

A shirtless Cillian. Sweat glistened on his muscles as his fists connected with a heavy bag. Each hit made the bag shake and swing.

There was a beauty to it, the way he moved around the black form, bobbing and weaving between each punch. But I could also see the fury behind each connection, and beneath that, the pain.

My chest constricted as he leveled an especially vicious punch at the bag.

"This isn't the time, Hayden."

Cillian hadn't once looked away from the heavy bag, but of course, he knew I was there.

I took a deep breath and walked farther into the gym instead of retreating.

"Hayden," he growled.

"I'm not leaving."

Cillian's head snapped up. His eyes had bled completely black. "You're not?"

I swallowed hard. I guessed an alpha wasn't used to getting the *no* sort of answers. "I'm not."

"Why. Not?" Cillian gritted out as he prowled toward me.

I squared my shoulders, a ridiculous attempt to stand my ground when Cillian was over a foot taller than me. "Because you're hurting."

He came up short, stopping in his tracks. "Little Flame..."

There was so much pain in those two words, so much unspoken emotion.

I closed the distance between us, taking one of his hands. I slowly unwound the black wraps on his fists. When the material fell to the ground, I could see that the flesh on his knuckles was torn.

I moved on instinct, lifting his hand to my mouth and brushing my lips across the torn skin.

"Careful. I'm not in control right now."

I lifted my gaze to Cillian's. "Then lose control with me."

Chapter Twelve

Hayden

Cillian's dark green eyes swirled black again. "Bad idea, Little Flame."

I stared up at him, pressing closer. "You won't hurt me."

"You don't know that," he growled, but his arms wrapped around me, his hands squeezing my ass.

"I do," I said, pouring all the certainty I could into my voice.

Cillian hardened against me, and my thighs clenched instinctively. He needed this. *I* needed this.

I summoned every ounce of bravery I had and slid my hand into Cillian's workout shorts. I wrapped my fingers around his length and stroked.

The growl he let loose was pure pleasure.

The sound emboldened me. I stroked again. He felt like silk wrapped around steel. Each pass of my hand sent waves of heat through me.

"Enough!" Cillian barked.

I released him, stepping back.

Another growl left his lips, darker this time. "You want to play, Little Flame?"

"Yes," I breathed.

Cillian bent down then, picking up the discarded hand wrap. He prowled toward me, a predator stalking his prey.

He grabbed my wrist and jerked me against him. "So pretty. So innocent. Love making you blush. Let's see all the places that pretty blush spreads."

In a flash, Cillian had both my wrists in one hand and had backed me up against the heavy bag. He lifted my arms, tying my wrists to the bag's chains with the wraps. The moment he was done, he stepped back, breathing ragged.

I tested the bindings. Tight but not horribly so. Just the slightest bit of discomfort.

"Safe word," he gritted out.

"Red," I whispered.

"Slow down?"

"Yellow."

Cillian's eyes sparked and swirled. "And right now?"

"Green." The sound was part word, part breath. But it was all Cillian needed.

He stalked toward me, unsheathing the claws on his right hand. I sucked in a breath but didn't say a word. In one fluid motion, he shredded the tank top I'd changed into after my shower. It fell to the floor in a flutter of fabric.

"Kind of wasteful, Cill," I muttered.

His eyes narrowed. "Talking back, Little Flame? Do you need a punishment?"

My core clenched, wetness and heat pooling between my legs.

"You like that. You might just be perfect." Cillian unsheathed the claws on his left hand, too. He swiped both hands down the sides of my sweatpants. They fell to the floor, too.

"I really liked those."

Cillian's lips twitched. "I'll buy you another pair."

He rose, stepping in close and cupping me between my legs. The only thing between us was the lace of my thong.

A low, rumbling growl left his chest. "Soaked." His gaze swept over my face. "Aching?"

My throat worked as I swallowed. "Yes."

A devious smile spread across Cillian's face. "Can you be a good girl and stay very still?"

My heart hammered against my ribs as my breaths came faster. I nodded.

He gripped me harder. "Words."

"Yes."

The grin was back, but then his hand was gone. His fingers twisted in the side of my thong, and he tore it clean off my body.

Cillian took a step back, his gaze running over my naked form. "You always walk around the house with no bra?"

My nipples pebbled under his focus. "Um, when I'm not going anywhere."

Cillian ran a finger under his lower lip as he took me in. "Good to know."

He moved toward me then, that panther-like grace in full effect. I gulped as he dropped to his knees. "Let's see how still you can stay."

Oh, hell.

Cillian's fingers trailed up the inside of my leg. "If you stay still, I'll let you come. If you don't, I'll take you over my knee."

A whimper left my lips.

Cillian's gaze jerked to my face. "Would you like that, Little Flame? Me spanking you until your ass turns a delicious shade of pink?"

More wetness pooled at the apex of my thighs. I tried to press them together, but Cillian's palm came down on my inner thigh.

"Still," he commanded, that alpha authority bleeding into his voice. "Don't hide from me."

Cillian widened my stance, my center on display for him.

"Glistening. Beautiful." He looked up at me as my face flamed. "This is nothing to be embarrassed about, Hayden. It just shows me how much you want this. Want *me*."

I nodded slowly.

His fingers parted me, and I sucked in a breath as they slid inside. I couldn't help my eyes falling closed on the delicious stretch.

"Open," Cillian ordered. "Eyes on me."

My lids flew open, my gaze finding his. That dark green was practically black again. Cillian's fingers curled inside me, and my legs trembled.

Cillian stroked that spot that had everything inside me vibrating. "Don't come."

"I don't know if I can control that," I admitted.

His eyes sparked. "You can, and you will."

I bit the inside of my cheek.

Cillian grinned and leaned forward. His tongue flicked across my clit, and I cried out as sensation ripped through me.

All Cillian did was slip another finger inside me.

I whimpered, my fingers tugging hard on the wraps around my wrists. The bite of pain helped me fight back the orgasm, but then Cillian's lips closed around the bundle of nerves. He worked my clit like an artist painting a masterpiece.

As his fingers stroked inside me, his tongue teased my hood, tempting it back until my most sensitive spot was exposed to him. "Don't come," he growled against my flesh.

I bit down on my cheek until the coppery tang of blood filled my mouth.

The tip of Cillian's tongue rolled around my clit, sending a wildfire blazing across my skin. My walls clamped down on his fingers, trying to get him to stop moving because I couldn't hold it back. Not anymore.

"I can't," I gasped.

"A little more. Hold it back," Cillian crooned as he pressed his fingers down.

Tears filled my eyes, spilling over from the sheer sensation overwhelming me. Pressure, so much of it, everywhere.

"So beautiful." Cillian's voice was a balm washing over me. "Taking it all. That's my good girl."

Everything in me shook. The chain rattled above my head with the force of it all.

"Let go. Come for me, Little Flame."

Cillian's lips closed around my clit, and he sucked hard as his fingers pressed firmly against my G-spot.

It was as if someone lit a chain of fireworks within, explosion after explosion of sensation, everything stretching outward. And I shattered, my vision tunneling as Cillian took everything I had.

My legs collapsed, and Cillian gripped me around the waist but didn't let up. Not until I was limp and barely conscious.

He stood, cradling me in one arm while he cut the binds with his other hand. He held me to him, nuzzling my neck. "My good girl. Always giving me everything I need."

Chapter Thirteen

Hayden

I was practically boneless as Cillian carried me up the stairs and toward his bedroom. I couldn't even be bothered by the fact that I was completely naked and anyone in the house could've seen me.

He laid me gently on the bed, pulling the covers up around me and brushing his lips across my temple. "Be right back."

I mumbled something incoherently, already slipping into that state between sleep and wakefulness. I heard the shower turn on. My body stirred a fraction, pushing me to follow Cillian into the shower, to give him a little of what he'd given me. But sleep tugged at me again.

I woke as the bed dipped behind me. Cillian's large form curved around my smaller one as he pulled me to him.

"I need to shower," I grumbled.

"Tomorrow." His breath tickled my ear.

I laced my fingers through his as they rested on my belly. "Are you okay?"

Cillian was quiet for a moment before he answered. "No. Not really."

An ache lit in my chest as I gripped his fingers tighter. "It seems like both you and Maddox have a history with the council."

Cillian's thumb swept back and forth across my belly, but he didn't speak.

I worried the corner of my lip, the darkness in the room making me brave. "I want to know you, Cill. That means opening up to each other and learning about each other—more than just the fact that we're mates, and that's that."

Cillian tugged me tighter against him. "I know you as more than my mate."

I huffed.

"You're obsessed with science and science puns, you try to help others, even when you shouldn't, and you want to be a doctor because, in some way, it'll give you a chance to save your parents."

I stilled, my body tensing. "How do you know that?"

Cillian traced a design on my stomach. "I pay attention, Little Flame. And I'm starving for any little piece of information you give us."

Rolling to face him, I strained to make out his features in the dark. "Don't you think I might feel the same way? But you're not nearly as easy to read."

Cillian's lips twitched. "That's by design."

"Cut a girl some slack."

His hand lifted, fingers tangling in my hair. "My father wasn't a good man."

My stomach twisted at his words. There was no emotion in Cillian's voice. It was simply empty. "How so?"

"He kidnapped my mother. Kept her prisoner in a dungeon and raped her repeatedly. I'm a child of those assaults."

I sucked in a painful breath. "Cillian…"

"She never made me feel that way, though. She loved me with everything she had. She finally convinced a guard to help me escape.

That guard knew that, eventually, my father would likely kill both me and her. He already had a political marriage in the works. I was nothing but a bastard son, a liability to his lineage."

Everything hurt. "You got out?"

He nodded. "The guard gave me a little cash. I ran to the nearest large city and lived on the streets."

"How old were you?"

"Twelve."

An image of a young Cillian scared and alone flashed in my mind. I couldn't stand it. I moved into him, pressing myself tight to his side and laying a hand over his chest. I needed to feel that steady beat of his heart against my palm. To remind myself that he was okay.

"I found other shifters. Stuck with a group of them. One told me about the council. Said that they were supposed to get involved if any dragon shifters, anywhere in the world, stepped out of line."

"So, you went to them," I surmised.

Cillian's heart beat faster, pounding against my hand. "I saved up for months. Finally got enough money for the bus fare to New York. Went to Nolan's office."

Everything inside me twisted into knots. "It didn't go well."

"He told me that there was no proof of my father's wrongdoings. I begged him to search the area I told him about, but he refused to do that to someone of my father's reputation. Patrick O'Connor was the king, after all. He led one of the largest dragon hordes in the world."

I wished I would've punched Nolan in the nose today. No, I wished I would have done so much worse.

"What did you do?" I whispered.

"I tried to go back. To get her out myself. But when I got there, I found out she'd already been killed. He ended her life as if she were nothing more than a piece of garbage to throw away."

Tears burned the backs of my eyes. "I'm so sorry."

Cillian's hand found the back of my neck and squeezed. "Me, too. I never should've left her. I should've stayed—"

"No." I put as much force behind the word as possible. "So you could've been killed, too? That's the last thing your mom would've wanted."

Even in the darkness, Cillian's eyes blazed. "She was alone."

"But she knew you were free. That gave her peace."

Cillian hauled me on top of him, pressing his face to my neck. I felt wetness there and knew he was crying. One of the strongest men I'd ever known, letting his tears fall for the woman who'd given him everything.

"I killed him. My father," Cillian said, voice rough. "I did it to protect my half brothers, but I would've done it, regardless. In cold blood, with no provocation."

I pulled back a fraction, wanting to see his eyes. "Do you think that's going to make me run?"

"It probably should," Cillian murmured. "I have a coldness in me. A cruelty. I needed it for survival."

I pressed up, straddling his lap and placing my hands on his chest. "Loving you means every part of you. I love that coldness and cruelty because they kept you alive. They brought you to me."

"Hayden," he croaked.

"I love you."

Cillian hardened against my core. "I don't know if I even know what that means, let alone if I'm capable of it."

My expression softened. "You love the people around you every single day. You'll trust it one day."

But until he did, I'd show him in other ways.

So that was exactly what I did.

Chapter Fourteen

Hayden

"You seem like you're in a better mood," Cáel said as he helped me into Easton's SUV.

"And Cill *definitely* seems like he's in a better mood," Knox said with a chuckle.

I fought the blush that rose to my cheeks, but it was no use.

Cáel grinned, pulling me onto his lap and nuzzling my neck. "I'm glad you guys worked some things out."

I pulled back, staring up at him. "You really are, aren't you?"

Cáel's hand trailed up my thigh. "He was upset yesterday. He needed you. I could feel his restlessness, but after you were with him, there was peace."

My brows pulled together. "You can feel each other?"

"It's more like a faint echo of a feeling," Knox explained. "It'll be stronger once we all bond with you."

Easton's fingers tightened on the wheel as he drove away from the house, but he didn't say a word.

I couldn't figure him out. Ever since the attack, he'd just gone quiet. He wasn't being an asshole anymore, but he wasn't warm and fuzzy either. I was starting to think I preferred the jerk. At least I knew what he was thinking then.

I glanced back at Knox. "Will I feel it, too?"

Knox grinned. "Every time there's heightened emotion or feeling. I heard it's great for—"

Easton smacked him, hard.

"Ow. What the hell?"

"Can we just chill on the sex talk before eight a.m.?" Easton grumbled.

I ducked my head. Of course, Easton didn't want to think about me and sex in the same sentence. Even if his body might want me, thanks to the mating urge, his brain and heart didn't.

"When are you going to pull your head out of your ass?" Knox growled.

"Excuse me for not wanting to show up to Mad's class with a raging hard-on," Easton shot back.

My stomach cramped. I hadn't seen Maddox since the council's visit yesterday. He'd disappeared and hadn't returned home, as far as I could tell. The cramping turned to nausea as I wondered where he'd stayed last night.

Cáel nuzzled the side of my neck. "What's wrong, Little One?"

"Nothing," I whispered.

"I can smell your anxiety."

"That's cheating," I groused.

Cáel grinned against my skin. "I like all the things your body tells me."

I squirmed on his lap, and Cáel instantly hardened against my ass. *Shit.*

He only grinned wider. "Tell me what's wrong."

Easton's focus remained on the road, but Knox glanced into the back seat, waiting for my answer.

I finally blew out a breath. These nosy dragons wouldn't let up until they knew what was bothering me. "I'm worried about Maddox. And I was, um, wondering where he stayed last night."

Understanding dawned on Knox's face. "He has a tiny cabin up in the mountains. He goes there sometimes when we get to be too much for him. But he always goes alone. None of us have even been there."

The relief that coursed through me was both welcome and embarrassing. I didn't have any rights to Maddox. He'd made it clear that he wasn't going there with me. How painful would it be if he and Easton decided to move on with different women? Would I still feel the pull toward them?

Cáel nuzzled my neck again as Easton pulled onto campus. "It's going to be okay."

I wished I could believe him.

Easton swung into a spot near the science building, our two enforcers, Pete and Terry, parking next to us. Cáel opened the door and lifted me out. Knox was waiting.

He pulled me into his arms and kissed me deeply. I couldn't help the moan that slipped free as his tongue stroked mine. He growled into my mouth. And as he pulled back, his eyes flashed gold. "I missed you."

My heart squeezed, and I wrapped my arms around Knox's waist. He was the one who always seemed to have it together, like he didn't need me as much. But maybe that wasn't true. "How about we do something, just you and me, after school?"

Knox's entire face lit at my suggestion. "You and me?"

He kissed me again and then slid his arm around my shoulders. I reached toward Cáel to take my backpack, but he just shook his head. "I got it."

I opened my mouth to argue and then snapped it shut. I'd never win anyway.

We headed for the science building, even though Cáel and Knox didn't have class there this morning. It had become routine for them to accompany me wherever I was going before leaving for their own classes. But the truth was, I didn't mind it. I liked having as many of my guys near as possible.

My guys.

A few weeks ago, the thought would've been preposterous. Now it felt normal. More than that, it felt *right.*

Easton strode ahead, opening the door. The building was full of students heading to their various classes.

Delaney and Bella strode by as Delaney sent me a look that should've fried me on the spot.

"Looks like she didn't get the message yesterday," Easton muttered.

Knox glanced at him. "She has Mad's class with you guys, right?"

Easton nodded.

"Keep a lookout," Knox ordered. "I don't like how she's fixated on Hayden."

Easton jerked his head in a nod.

We wound our way through the halls until a guy stepped into our path. He licked his lips in an exaggerated motion. "How do I get in line for a piece? Or do you require payment?"

One moment he was in front of me, and the next he was pinned against the wall, three feet in the air. Cáel pressed his forearm to the guy's throat. "Say. That. Again."

Everyone in the hallway froze, all stopping to stare at the show.

"Fuck, man. I was kidding," he wheezed.

Easton strode up next to Cáel, casual as could be. "Does it look like anyone's laughing?"

"N-n-no."

"Put him down, Cáel. I'm pretty sure he already shit his pants. I can smell it," Easton said with disgust.

Some of the students around us snickered, and the guy flushed.

"No," Cáel grunted.

"Let him go this once, and if he says something again, I'll let you gut him like a fish," Easton said casually, as if he didn't have a care in the world.

The guy's face went from red to sickly pale. "I-I won't say anything. Swear."

Cáel growled low but released his hold, and the guy crumbled to a heap on the floor. I was pretty sure he was crying.

"Shit, man," the redheaded friend of Knox's muttered as he walked up. "What'd Erik do to Cáel?"

Knox's grip on me was just shy of pain, and I saw that he was struggling for control. I quickly slipped a hand under his tee, pressing my palm to his back. "I'm okay," I whispered.

Knox swallowed hard. "He said some shit about Hayden."

Jason's eyes widened, and then he glanced at the fallen guy. "Real dumb move, Erik. Tell all your soccer buddies that Hayden's off-limits."

Erik scrambled to his feet, flipping Jason off but jogging down the hallway.

Jason sent me a grin. "Some guys have no manners. *I,* on the other hand—"

A hand came out to smack him across the back of the head. Their friend, Frank, shoved him aside. "Did you not just see shit-his-pants-Erik get his ass literally handed to him?"

Cáel stalked around them and into my space, breathing hard. His white-blond hair swung around him with the force of his agitation.

The entire hallway went deadly quiet.

I released my hold on Knox and lifted my hands to Cáel's cheeks. I pulled his face down to mine so that our foreheads pressed together. "I'm good. It's just an idiot saying stupid stuff."

"He can't talk about you."

My mouth curved. "I have a feeling he won't ever again."

I wanted to kiss Cáel so badly. I knew it was a bad idea. People thought I was with Knox. There were rumors of the other guys but nothing more. If I kissed him, there would be proof. I'd be branded with that scarlet A. But Cáel needed me right then. So...

Fuck it.

And the whispers around us turned to roars.

Hayden

PETE AND TERRY FLANKED ME THE MOMENT I STEPPED out of my English lit class. They'd been on edge all day. And not for no reason.

I'd been right about the kiss with Cáel. The entire campus was buzzing. The reaction was a mixture. A fair amount of disgust. A healthy dose of jealousy. And more than a few crude comments, always whispered when none of the guys were around.

Wren gave me a small wave as she headed down the hallway, the action making her hair swing and exposing the scar on her cheek. She glanced warily at the two enforcers. "You'll be okay?"

I nodded. "Not going to let a bunch of prudes get me down."

Her lips gave the faintest twitch. "Good. See you tomorrow?"

"I'll be the one wearing the scarlet A."

Wren just shook her head and took off down the hall.

Pete, Terry, and I made our way through the half-crowded halls. I ignored everyone in my path until someone stepped di-

I came up short, my gaze jerking upward, and then I sighed with relief. "You're a sight for sore eyes."

And what a sight he was. Dark-wash jeans that hugged his hips and skimmed his muscular thighs. A white T-shirt that hinted at the defined muscles I knew lay below.

Knox took the backpack from my shoulder and slung it over his own. Then he pulled me to him, brushing his lips across mine. "We need more classes together. I missed you all day."

I melted into him. "I'm starting to wonder if I can switch to online classes."

He grimaced. "That bad today?"

"Not the greatest." I pulled back. "Do *not* tell Cáel."

The last thing we needed was him getting expelled because he slit someone's throat for scowling at me.

"I solemnly swear," Knox promised. He kissed me again. "But I'm really sorry. We don't have to do anything today. We can just go home and—"

"No. I could use a little dose of normal."

Knox grinned at me. "Good. I was thinking I could take you shopping, and then we could grab dinner."

My face scrunched. "Shopping?"

He chuckled as he wrapped an arm around me and guided me toward the building's exit. "I thought girls loved shopping."

"I think that gene skipped me." Maybe it was just that I'd never had any practice.

"Cill mentioned that you'll need something for the cocktail party on Saturday. I thought you might feel more comfortable if you picked it out yourself."

My stomach pitched. The cocktail party. The fucking council making me meet the hordes of their choosing.

"If I wear a garbage bag, maybe the other dragons will leave right away."

Knox pressed a kiss to my temple. "You'd still be the most beautiful thing they'd ever seen."

My mouth curved. "I think you're biased."

"Never." He pulled me tighter against him. "We don't have to go shopping. I just thought you might want to have that bit of control."

"No, you're right. It might help. Like armor."

"Exactly."

I stretched up on my tiptoes to kiss the underside of his jaw. "Thanks for knowing me."

"I'm a quick study."

As we stepped out into the sunshine, we almost collided with someone.

"Sorry," Knox said.

Professor Brent glared at us, his expression colder than I'd ever seen it. That frigid stare landed on me for a beat more than was appropriate, but my advisor didn't say a word.

Finally, Knox simply guided us around him and toward the familiar X5. "I really don't like that guy."

"You and me both," I muttered.

Knox opened the passenger door for me. "You can request an advisor change."

"I'm going to as soon as I'm done with his psych class. I don't want him to give me a bad grade because he's pissed I asked for someone else."

Knox's mouth thinned. "We've got months left in the semester."

"I can deal with him until then." I hoped I could, anyway.

"Tell me if it gets worse."

I bit the inside of my cheek and nodded. I didn't trust my voice not to give away my lie.

Knox closed the door, letting the enforcers know where we were headed so that they could follow. In a matter of seconds, he was behind the wheel, and we were on our way toward downtown.

I glanced over at Knox, just taking in his beauty for a moment.

The light brown hair with golden highlights. The green eyes with flecks of gold. The jaw that could cut glass.

"You're staring."

I grinned. "I like staring at you."

Knox took my hand, weaving our fingers together and resting it on his thigh. The action felt so normal. So comforting.

"How are things with you and Easton?"

It was the wrong thing to ask. Knox's easygoing expression turned stormy.

"They're fine." But the words came through gritted teeth.

I squeezed Knox's fingers. "I don't want to be the reason for you two fighting."

"You're not. East being a stubborn ass is the reason for us fighting."

"He's scared, Knox. You said that yourself."

"He might be, but at some point, we have to stop excusing his fucked-up behavior because of it." Knox swung into a parking spot, his gaze coming to me. The flecks of gold were brighter, swirling in the green depths. "You almost *died* because of him. I can't just sweep that under the rug."

"Knox—"

"I can't, Hayden."

I let out a long breath. "Okay. Just hear him out when you're ready to talk. Promise me?"

Knox's jaw worked back and forth. "All right."

I leaned over and kissed his cheek. "Thank you."

"He doesn't deserve your loyalty," Knox grumbled.

"I'm not doing it for him. I'm doing it for you."

Knox stilled, his eyes burning. "Don't know how I got so lucky to find you."

"Me either," I whispered.

A door slammed next to us, breaking the moment.

Knox kissed me again. "Come on. Let's go get you a hell of a dress."

Chapter Sixteen

Hayden

KNOX SLID OUT OF THE SUV WITH THAT EFFORTLESS EASE he always had. There was this comfortable confidence he wore like a second skin, and it was addicting. A moment later, he was opening my door.

"Such a gentleman."

He grinned, taking my hand. "Well, this is our first real date."

I blinked up at him. "Have we seriously not even been on a date?"

So much had happened over the past few weeks, but I wasn't sure a *real* date was among them.

Knox tugged me toward a shop. "I'm not counting bringing you hot chocolate that got interrupted by Easton being an ass. Or sandwiches that got interrupted by Maddox freaking you out."

I bit my bottom lip to keep from laughing. "Your game really was constantly being ruined."

"No fucking kidding. So, we've had near-death experiences, the reveal of a supernatural world's existence, and the discovery that you're our soulmate. But no first date."

I couldn't hold in the laugh this time, and damn, it felt good. Because when Knox listed it all out like that, it was ridiculous.

"So, I am finally taking my girl on a date."

I stilled as he grabbed hold of the door. "I like the sound of that."

Knox smiled at me. "A date?"

"*My girl.*"

His green-and-gold eyes heated. "Careful. I'll forget all the date nonsense and just take us to a hotel instead."

Warmth pooled low in my belly. "I wouldn't be opposed—"

Knox kissed me fast and hard. "No. I'm spoiling you, feeding you, and then I'll fuck you seven ways from Sunday."

This time, the laugh did bubble out of me. "So romantic."

"Damn straight." He opened the door, holding it for me.

As soon as we entered, a woman hurried toward us. "Mr. Gallagher, so wonderful to see you again."

"Hi, Sharee."

The middle-aged woman's gaze flicked to me. "Are you and your brothers in need of a wardrobe update?"

Knox shook his head. "My girlfriend needs a dress for a cocktail party this weekend. Hayden, this is Sharee. Sharee, Hayden."

That warmth that had flickered to life earlier, swirled and spread. *Girlfriend* was almost as good as *my girl.*

The woman's expression lit with pure joy at the announcement. She clasped her hands together. "This is just wonderful news." Her gaze swept to me. "I'm assuming Hayden is who we placed the earlier order for?"

Knox nodded.

"Good. Then we have all her sizes." Sharee's smile grew. "Can't imagine anything that wouldn't look stunning on you, dear. Do you want my help to pull some things, or would you like to browse first?"

For some reason, the woman's kindness had me fighting back tears. Maybe because it seemed like most people weren't thrilled with my involvement with Knox and the guys. Maybe because so many people had been downright mean today. But I found myself having to swallow down the emotion clogging my throat.

"Thank you so much. I think I'll look around first."

Sharee patted my shoulder. "I like a woman who knows what she wants. I'll be at the register in the back if you need me."

"Thanks, Sharee," Knox said.

The woman left us to browse.

"She's really nice," I whispered.

"She orders everything clothes-wise for us. I think we keep her in business."

I chuckled at that. "I can't imagine there's a ton of call for"—I picked up a tag—"Chanel in Ember Hollow."

Knox shook his head. "Probably not."

We wandered through the racks. I had to admit, the pieces were stunning. But all the price tags made me blanch.

"This might be too much," I murmured.

Knox took my shoulders. "We have more money than we'll ever be able to spend. Let us take care of you." He lowered his voice. "Our dragons need it as much as we do."

I bit my bottom lip, glancing back at a lavender silk creation.

Knox followed my line of sight and stalked toward it, pulling it off the rack. "It would look gorgeous on you with your eyes."

The four-figure price tag made me nauseous.

He let out a low growl. "You're trying it on."

I stuck my tongue out at him. "Bossy."

"When it comes to your happiness, yes."

Knox guided me toward the dressing rooms in the middle of the store and tugged me inside one, closing the door behind us.

"You can't come in here with me."

He arched a brow. "Interesting. Looks like I already am."

"Sharee is out there," I hissed.

A bell jingled, and I heard Sharee greeting another customer.

"Knox!"

He simply leaned against the wall and crossed his arms over his wide chest. "Yes?"

"Are all dragons this stubborn?"

His lips twitched. "Not sure if that's a genetic trait or not."

"I think it is," I groused as I tugged my sweater and shirt over my head and tossed it at him.

He laughed as it smacked him in the face.

I shimmied out of my jeans and hurried to slip into the dress before Knox could really get us into trouble. The fabric felt like heaven against my skin. Like the softest glove. I pulled it up and over my shoulders. Reaching behind me, I tried to zip it—

"Let me." Knox's voice was deeper as he stepped behind me.

Goose bumps rose on my arms as he swept my hair out of the way. Painfully slowly, he zipped me into the garment. Then his eyes met mine in the mirror.

It was as if I saw myself through his gaze before I even took in my own reflection. I saw the heat, the lust, the reverence. Pulling my focus away from Knox, I took myself in.

My lips parted on a whispered inhale. The dress was perfect. It hugged my curves with a ruched pattern to the fabric. The skirt hit at my knees, and the neckline only gave the smallest peek at the swells of my cleavage, but the material hinted at everything below. It made me feel sexy and powerful, but someone to be respected, too.

"I feel beautiful," I whispered.

Knox's eyes blazed as he bent to kiss my neck. "Most stunning creature I've ever laid eyes on. It was made for you."

"It's too much—"

"No. It's just enough."

Knox's fingers came back to the zipper, and they slid it down.

He knelt.

"Step out." His voice was gruff, coated in sandpaper.

I did as he asked.

Knox laid the dress carefully on a tufted ottoman and gazed up at me. "I need to taste you."

Wetness pooled between my thighs.

Knox's eyes flared, and he groaned. "You smell like heaven."

"You can smell *that*?"

He grinned. "Heightened senses, remember?"

I cursed.

Knox's hands came to my hips. "Still."

I couldn't help but obey.

"That's my girl."

More heat. More wetness.

Knox's fingers latched on to the sides of my thong, and he slowly slid them down my legs. Then he leaned forward and inhaled. "Pure heaven."

My thighs trembled.

He lifted one leg, placing it farther apart from the other. Then his hands went to my ass, squeezing, kneading. His hooded gaze met mine. "I can't wait to take you here."

My mouth fell open.

"Love that innocent shock."

And then he devoured. There was no warning with Knox. He ate me like a man starved. His tongue drove inside, making me nearly fall straight over.

I grabbed on to Knox's shoulders as his tongue curled inside me. I couldn't help the soft whimper that escaped me.

Knox squeezed my ass harder.

I bit the inside of my cheek to keep from making more sounds.

One hand slid between my legs as his tongue circled my clit. Knox thrust two fingers inside me, and my mouth fell open on a pant.

As they curled, my breaths came faster. Knox teased that bundle of nerves, coaxing it out to stand at attention. My heart hammered, and my fingers were sure to leave bruises on his shoulders.

The tip of Knox's tongue flicked my clit, and I shattered.

Knox held me behind my legs, his face still buried between my thighs, as his fingers worked me through every wave of my orgasm.

I struggled to catch my breath as I came down, my body twitching with aftershocks.

Knox slowly pulled his fingers from my body. His eyes locked with mine, and then he licked those fingers clean.

My lips parted.

He looked up at me. "I was wrong. You've never been more beautiful than you are right now."

A throat cleared outside the dressing room. "Everything okay in there? My other customer thought someone might be hurt. Heard a little moaning."

There was pure amusement in Sharee's voice, but I wanted to die. I jumped, trying to find my underwear. "We're good," I squeaked.

"Better than good, Sharee," Knox called.

She giggled. "That's what I thought."

I glared at Knox. "I'm going to murder you."

Chapter Seventeen

Hayden

I skimmed my hands over the silky fabric. The feel of it was otherworldly. The softest thing I'd ever felt.

Surveying my reflection in the mirror, I almost didn't recognize myself. I hadn't done the prom thing after my one disastrous foray into dating. I certainly hadn't been invited to any weddings or galas. So, this was the fanciest I'd ever looked.

Knox had been right. Having a dress that I'd picked, one that I felt confident in, helped. I'd taken painstaking time with my makeup and hair. I'd rimmed my eyes in a purple so dark it was almost black. But my irises seemed to recognize the undertones, and the violet in them blazed brighter. I'd coated my lips in a sheer light pink that made them look plumper.

I'd spent at least an hour wielding the fancy new curling iron in my bathroom. I'd taken tiny sections, weaving the hair around the barrel. The effect was full, voluminous curls trailing down my back.

Any other time, I'd simply marvel at the miracle I'd created

At feeling truly beautiful. But not tonight. Not when I would have to face the council. Countless unfamiliar dragons.

The last few days had passed in a blur of catching up on studying, trying to avoid Professor Brent, and wondering where Maddox was. He still hadn't returned to class or home. As much as he didn't want it, I was worried about him.

A knock sounded on the open closet door.

"Hayden, we'll be leaving in ten minutes. Are you—"

Cillian's deep voice cut off as he took me in. I met his eyes in the mirror. His dark green irises deepened to almost black.

"What's wrong?" Knox asked, hurrying in behind him. But he drew up short as I turned around.

Cáel barreled in behind them. "Is she okay?"

He, too, came to a jerky halt, his pale blue eyes going wide. "Little One," he breathed.

"Stunning," Cillian growled.

Knox grinned, but there was a simmering heat beneath it. "Second favorite outfit ever."

My cheeks heated, remembering Knox on his knees, gazing up at me.

"Is it too much?"

Cillian strode toward me, his hand cupping the juncture of my jaw and neck. "You're perfect."

"Too perfect for these assholes," Cáel grumbled.

I smiled at that, his words easing some of the tension thrumming through me. "Walk me through it?"

Cillian jerked his head in a nod, releasing me as he stepped back.

For the first time, I really took them all in. God, they were breathtaking. Cillian was in his usual black suit and black dress shirt. They fit him as if the designer had crafted the garments just for him. And maybe they had. He had just a hint of stubble along his sharp jaw, and his hair was freshly buzzed.

Knox wore a dark blue suit that made the green in his eyes

pop. It accentuated his broad shoulders and muscular chest. His hair was perfectly styled in an artful disarray. My fingers itched to run through it.

Cáel had taken the dress code and made it his own. While he wore black dress pants and a gray button-down, he'd thrown his signature leather jacket over it instead of a suit jacket. The tattoos decorating his hands, neck, and sides of his head seemed to pop all the more.

They were all beautiful. And they were mine.

"Hayden?" Cillian prodded, concern lacing his tone.

I gave myself a little shake. "Sorry. What?"

"You went somewhere else," Knox said, brow furrowing.

I flushed. "I, uh, was just admiring the three of you. You look very handsome tonight."

Cáel grinned at me, the same smile that looked slightly deranged from lack of use. "Handsome, huh?"

"Shut up," I grumbled. "I'm allowed to look."

"Our Little Flame does love to watch. It's something we need to remember," Cillian all but purred.

Knox muttered a curse. "Do we have to go to this thing? I can think of a hundred better ways to spend our time."

His eyes went hooded, the gold in them sparking.

Cillian squared his shoulders. "We need to get it over with, or the council will just stay on our backs."

My stomach flipped. "I want it done. Tell me what I'll have to do."

Cillian leaned against the elaborate dresser in the middle of the massive closet. "The council will have pulled a selection of hordes. My guess is around five."

"Whichever five offered them the highest bribes," Cáel muttered.

Cillian sent him a quelling look. "You will have to shake each of their hands. The theory is to find out if you are their true mate."

"But we already know I'm *your* true mate."

The set of Cillian's jaw hardened. "We do, but the council will say they're just being thorough. You also always have the option of rejecting us and choosing a different horde."

Cáel shifted, anxiety flashing across his expression.

My chest squeezed, and I moved quickly toward him. Wrapping my arms around his waist, I gazed up into those pale blue eyes. "I don't want anyone but you, this bond. Please know that."

I'd fallen for all three of them, and I couldn't ignore the way my heart tugged toward the two others, even if they didn't feel the same. As complicated as this was, I wouldn't give it up for anything.

Cáel's eyes sparked with silver. "I don't want you to go tonight."

"Me neither," I said honestly. "But we need to. You'll be with me the whole time."

Cáel simply grunted and hauled me against his chest, holding me tightly.

I listened to the steady beat of his heart. It was truly one of my favorite sounds, the certainty of it, the vibrancy. I knew he could keep me safe.

Knox cleared his throat. "If we don't go soon, we'll be late."

Cáel growled at Knox.

I patted his chest and extricated myself from his hold. "Let's get this over with."

Cillian's eyes locked with mine. "Stick close to us tonight."

Like he needed to tell me that, but, still, I assured him, "I will."

We filed out of my bedroom and into the hallway. The guys led the way down the stairs, and when they parted, they revealed two more forms.

Easton and Maddox stood in the foyer, staring at me.

Easton's light brown hair hung down, spilling around his

shoulders. It had a natural wave to it that highlighted the gold weaving through. He wore a navy suit that fit him perfectly, and those golden-green eyes blazed as they took me in.

Maddox stood next to him, wearing a black suit with a maroon button-down. It made the golden hue of his skin look that much richer and his amber eyes that much brighter. But those eyes were glaring at me with such rage, I nearly stumbled back a step.

They flashed with gold. “Hell fucking no.”

Chapter Eighteen

Hayden

Knox stalked toward Maddox, giving him a swift shove. "What the hell's the matter with you?"

"Me?" Maddox snapped. "What's wrong with all of you? Dressing her like a whore just ready for the taking?"

My face flamed as my shoulders curved in on themselves. All the feelings of confidence and of feeling beautiful slipped away.

Cáel moved before anyone had a chance to say a word. His fist flew through the air and cracked into Maddox's jaw. Maddox's head snapped to the side as he stumbled back a few steps.

"What the fuck, Cáel?" Maddox bellowed, holding his jaw.

Cáel charged again, but Knox and Cillian caught him before he could do any damage. He struggled against their hold. "You don't talk about our *mate* that way."

Maddox's gaze sliced to me. The action had me wrapping my arms around my middle, wishing I already had a jacket on to cover up with. The moment his eyes connected with mine, his face went carefully blank.

"You should've dressed her in a damned nun's habit," he spat, charging out the door.

I squeezed my arms tighter around my middle. I didn't think I'd ever heard Maddox curse until tonight. This whole thing had him unraveling. The council, the cocktail party, me.

"You look beautiful, Hayden." Easton's words were so low I almost didn't hear them.

My gaze jerked to his. Easton's expression was still carefully masked, but there was something brewing underneath, something I couldn't quite identify.

"Th-thank you," I mumbled.

He nodded quickly, then slipped out the front door.

Knox stared after his brother, but the moment the door shut, he crossed quickly to me. His hands framed my face, the calluses on his palms creating a pleasant shiver across my skin. "He's right. You're the most beautiful creature I've seen. But it's so much more. You're brave and strong and care for people, even when they don't deserve it."

He bent, his lips brushing mine. When he pulled back, his eyes had gone stormy. "We're with you, every step of the way."

Cillian cleared his throat, holding up a jacket that was the same color as my dress.

I glanced back at Knox in question.

He shrugged. "I had Sharee order it. You needed something warm."

"Of course, you did." I just shook my head and then kissed his cheek. "Thank you."

Cillian helped me into the jacket, and we headed out to the waiting limo. As I slid inside, I couldn't help but notice that Maddox and Easton were sitting as far away from me as possible. That fact made my stomach twist. But the truth was, I didn't have time to worry about their hang-ups. Not when I was about to face a council who wanted to manipulate me away from three men who would do anything for me, who made me feel cherished, and who made me feel like I had a home.

Knox sat on one side of me, Cáel on the other, and Cillian sat between us and Maddox and Easton. I had a feeling that his position was strategic. As if to confirm that, Cillian sent Maddox a look of warning. He simply turned his head to stare out the window into the night.

The limo started up, and we were on our way. No one talked during the car ride. I realized I didn't even know where we were going, but I guessed it didn't matter.

Before long, the limo slowed in front of what looked like a historic home. It had a sort of Victorian look, and the sign read *Ember Hollow Historical Society*. Any other time, I would've been excited to check out what artifacts the place might hold, but not tonight.

Everything in me vibrated as Knox climbed out of the limo and offered me a hand. I took it, sliding out after him. The night wrapped around us, the stars twinkling up above in the clear sky. I wished I could just disappear into that sky.

Cáel flanked my other side, moving in close. His heat was a reassurance I needed.

Cillian strode to the front of our group as Easton and Maddox took up the rear. I didn't look at the last two. I wasn't sure I could take another of Maddox's glares.

There was a series of expensive-looking vehicles parked in the lot to the side of the home, along with another few limos lining the street. Everyone else was here.

Knox wove his fingers through mine, squeezing. "We're with you."

My throat constricted. "I know."

And that was a gift I hadn't had in so long. I wasn't sure that Knox could know just how much it meant.

"Anyone makes a move you don't like, I'll snap their neck," Cáel growled.

I couldn't help it. I laughed.

"Showing your love via murder?" I asked.

He grinned down at me with a twisted smile. "Always." Then the curve of his lips fell away. "I don't know exactly what love is, but I know that you make me feel. I've been numb for so long; it's just been easier that way. But with you...I feel again."

Tears built in my eyes, and I leaned into Cáel. "I love you. More than you'll ever know."

He bent down, taking my mouth in a slow kiss.

When he pulled back, it was to find that the rest of the guys were watching us. Knox had a look of sheer joy on his face. Cillian, smug pride. Easton, longing maybe? It was covered so quickly that I couldn't be sure. But Maddox wore rage again, so much that it hurt my skin.

I quickly looked away. "We should go."

I started walking. The guys surrounded me, Cillian leading the way.

As we entered the house, Fionn walked forward to greet us. He extended a hand to Cillian, holding a drink in the other. "And here I was, starting to worry that you'd run away with our little dragon."

Cillian's jaw hardened as he shook Fionn's hand. "We'd never go against the council's wishes."

Fionn chuckled, low and rich. "Why do I find that hard to believe?" He glanced at me. "May I take your jacket, Hayden?"

"I've got it," Knox hurried to say, sliding the coat off my shoulders and handing it to a staff member who had miraculously appeared.

Fionn's gaze swept over me, mischief in his dark eyes. "Come this way. Everyone's through here."

He led us into a massive formal living room that had been transformed for the occasion. Whatever furniture that had been in the space was removed and replaced with sporadically placed tall cocktail tables, and a bar was set up against the far wall.

The moment I stepped into the space, I felt eyes on me. So

many it had me wanting to shrink back and hide. But I squared my shoulders, summoning every ounce of bravery I had.

But that bravery died the moment a familiar face stepped into view.

The reddish-brown hair and dead eyes had my stomach twisting as Hal Corbett sneered at Easton. "I'm surprised you and your brother are here. Everyone knows your line isn't cut out for a mate. You could end up murdering everyone around you."

I sucked in a sharp breath as Knox moved toward his brother, knowing his move before Easton even made it. But it was too late.

Easton lunged.

Chapter Nineteen

Hayden

THANKFULLY, CÁEL WAS QUICKER, CATCHING HOLD of Easton's suit jacket and jerking him back. "Don't."

Hal laughed, but there was an ugly twist to the sound. "So touchy."

"You'll get what's coming to you, Corbett," Easton spat, his breathing ragged.

Hal's eyes narrowed. "Is that a threat on neutral territory?"

Shit. Shit. Shit. This was bad. So very bad. If one of my bond made a move in violence, the council might have cause to remove me from their protection.

I darted forward, slipping my arm through Easton's and gazing up at him. "Can you take me outside for a moment? I'm feeling a little flushed."

Easton was so shocked by my presence and touch that it seemed to steal the edge of his anger.

I squeezed his arm. "Please?"

"Sure," he muttered.

I tugged him quickly toward a hallway as people muttered

behind us. I had no idea where I was going, but I hoped I could find a way to a backyard or something. A waiter pulled up short as he saw us.

"Backyard?" I asked.

The waiter nodded quickly. "There's a patio. Make a right at the end of the hall."

"Thank you." But I didn't stop. I worried if I did, Easton might head back and deck Hal Corbett.

When I caught sight of the French doors, I breathed a tiny sigh of relief. Opening one, I led us through it.

The cold night air was a balm to the anxiety ripping through me. I released my hold on Easton, but he stayed close, staring down at me.

"Are you okay?" he asked gruffly.

"That was going to be my question."

Easton's gaze bored into mine as he mulled over his words. "No," he finally admitted.

My breath left me on a whoosh of air. "Me neither."

Pain twisted Easton's features. "I'm so sorry, Hayden. I'm sorry he hurt you. I'm sorry *I* hurt you."

My heart hammered against my ribs. "Knox told me what happened to your family."

That had Easton taking a step back, his face closing down.

"Please, don't," I begged. "Don't shut me out. I'd rather have you barking your insults at me than that."

Easton shook his head, scrubbing a hand over his jaw. "It was easier that way, wasn't it?"

One corner of my mouth kicked up. "Never thought I'd be wishing for someone to call me a piece of ass."

Easton winced. "I'm the ass."

"Not going to argue with you there."

He sighed, turning to face the immaculate gardens that led to thick forests. "I never want to turn into my older brother."

My heart squeezed. I could feel the fear in those words. "You won't."

Easton shook his head. "You don't know that. Ryan was just like us. Loved his family, his friends. He was *funny*. So full of life. So *normal*."

"What happened?" I asked softly. Knox had only told me that Ryan's mate had passed away, but none of the details.

Easton's jaw worked back and forth. "Ryan's mate was a dragon, but she didn't have the ability to shift. That's what happens to a lot of females of our species."

I wasn't sure why that mattered, but I stayed quiet, hoping he would keep going.

"When we're injured, shifting is what allows us to heal supernaturally."

My stomach twisted, dreading where this was going.

Easton's throat worked as he swallowed. "They were coming home from a concert, and a drunk driver T-boned them on Julie's side of the SUV. She didn't have a prayer. She was pinned inside the vehicle, and by the time Ryan got her out, she was barely breathing. Had she been a dragon, she could've shifted and healed herself. The driver was passed out, and there were no other humans around."

"But she couldn't."

Easton shook his head. "Ryan watched her die on the side of the road all because some idiot got behind the wheel drunk."

Tears filled my eyes. I knew what it was like to watch someone you loved fade in front of your eyes. I wouldn't wish it on my worst enemy. "I'm so sorry."

"It changed him. He went dark. Shut us all out. I knew we were in trouble when the driver turned up dead a couple of months later."

My stomach churned. I didn't blame Ryan for seeking vengeance, but I knew it wouldn't stop the pain.

"But he didn't stop there," Easton went on. "He went after the bartender that served the driver, then the owner of the bar. Finally, there was no one left for him to blame, so he turned it all on himself. His mind shattered. We tried to intervene…"

"And that turned him on you," I surmised.

Easton nodded. "He drugged us at dinner and set the house on fire. But he must've underestimated my and Knox's weight. We were growing fast back then. We woke up to smoke. We tried to get our sister and our parents, but they were already gone."

I had to move then, couldn't hear Easton's pain and not touch him. I crossed into his space, taking his hand in mine. "I'm so sorry. I wish I could take all the pain."

He stared down at me, eyes glittering in the moonlight. "Do you see now? You *terrify* me, Hayden. You already own me, and I've barely touched you."

My heart jerked in my chest. "Easton…"

His free hand lifted, his thumb ghosting across my bottom lip. "It would already ruin me if anything happened to you. The more I let myself into your orbit, the worse it gets."

Everything hurt because I could truly see Easton's fear. The reasons behind all of his assholish behavior. He was doing everything he could to push me away to protect himself. And here I was, trying to smash down those walls.

"But you make it so fucking hard." Easton's hand dropped to my neck, his fingers trailing over my pulse point, his mouth slowly moving closer.

My breath caught in my lungs. He was so close I swore I could already taste him. His scent, sea air and a hint of citrus, swirled around me.

The door behind us flew open with a bang.

Nolan glared through the night. "It's time to begin."

CHAPTER TWENTY

Hayden

EASTON JERKED UPRIGHT AT THE SOUND OF NOLAN'S VOICE, but to his credit, he didn't drop my hand. I knew it cost him. That fear was a living, breathing thing inside him, and he was battling it not to leave me alone.

"We'll be right there," I said as calmly as possible, even though my heart felt like it was ricocheting around my rib cage.

Nolan's eyes narrowed on us. "No. You'll come now."

Easton let out a low growl.

I squeezed his hand as hard as I could. "Lead the way."

Nolan let out a huff and started back inside.

We followed, but I slowed my pace enough to create distance between us and him. The last thing we needed was Easton snapping at him, too.

I took a deep breath as we stepped back into the living room. Our bond was waiting, their gazes coming to us as soon as we walked through the door.

Knox's eyes zeroed in on my and Easton's joined hands. Hope

flickered to life in his expression. I didn't begrudge him that hope, but I also didn't want him to be disappointed.

"We're ready for introductions. Please assemble," Nolan called to the small crowd.

Men clustered together in groups, and I realized that Cillian had been right. There were what looked to be five hordes. Hal and his bond were standing off to one side, and I didn't let myself look in that direction.

"You aren't seriously going to make her shake hands with the man who almost killed her," Easton spat.

Nolan sent him a droll look. "It sounds to me like it was an accident. One *you* caused. There's no reason why Hayden shouldn't meet the Corbett bond. Hal will be the next alpha, after all."

Easton's jaw tightened.

I squeezed his hand again. "I'll be okay."

I tried to make my words as believable as possible, but I wasn't sure how successful I was. I released Easton's hand and turned to Nolan. "Let's get this farce over with."

He glared at me, eyes sparking with anger. "Show some respect, girl."

I met his stare dead-on. "Respect is earned."

Cillian moved in then, squeezing my shoulder and pressing a kiss to the side of my head. "Good luck."

I pressed my lips together to keep from saying something I shouldn't.

Mona strode up then. She wore a slinky, maroon gown that accentuated her curves. "I'll escort her. We may need girl talk after all. Lots of delicious specimens in the room."

She laughed at her own joke as she linked arms with me. "If I didn't already have my own bond, I'd be making these boys jump through hoops for me. Make them promise you the world, Hayden. Jewels, travel, homes. It all can be yours."

I glanced up at her. "That's all pretty empty if they don't actually care for you."

Mona laughed again; this time it was a touch more real. "An idealist. Let's see how long that lasts."

She released me toward the first group.

I swallowed hard as the group of four men stared at me. Their expressions were hungry and more than a little dark. The largest man of the bunch stepped forward, his gaze roaming over my body before landing on my breasts. He didn't even bother to look at my face as he introduced himself.

"Julian, alpha of the Mercutio horde."

I took his hand. "Hayden, and my eyes are up here."

There was no hint of energy as we shook hands. I didn't feel faint, and my vision didn't tunnel.

Julian chuckled. "Fiery. I'd have fun breaking that spirit."

I jerked my hand out of his, turning to Mona. "I didn't feel a thing."

She nodded, motioning to the next group of men.

My back teeth ground together as I moved into their orbit.

An absolutely massive man stepped forward. He had a shaved head and a piercing through his septum. I nearly stumbled backward, but then a wide grin split his face. "Hayden, so pleased to meet you. I'm Roark."

"H-hi," I stammered.

"Told you that you'd scare the shit out of her, R. I should've gone," a leaner man chided him from behind.

Roark scowled at his friend. "Shut up."

I took a steadying breath. "Sorry, you are a little intimidating."

A hint of pink hit Roark's cheeks. "Comes in handy sometimes, not so much in others. Pleased to meet you."

He extended his hand, and I took it. There were no fireworks, and Roark immediately looked disappointed.

I squeezed his hand. "I'm sorry. You'll find your mate."

Roark gave me a kind smile. "You will, too."

Surprise flashed through me. "Didn't they tell you? I already have. They're over there." I inclined my head to my guys.

Anger flashed in Roark's eyes as he glared at Mona. "They neglected to share that tidbit of information."

Mona hurried forward. "She *thinks* she found her bond, but new dragons are easily confused."

She tugged me to the next group with a scowl. The next two hordes weren't nearly as warm as Roark's but not as creepy as Julian's. There were no fireworks with either.

Now, there was only one left. I swallowed hard as we moved toward Hal and his bond. He smiled at me, seeming to think that the action would charm me, but it came across as false and as smarmy as he was.

"Hayden, I'm so glad to finally meet you properly."

"You mean when you're not shooting fire into my chest?"

There were some curses and mutters around me.

Hal's jaw tightened. "You should be blaming Easton for that fuckup."

"We both know that there's only one person who should be blamed, and I'm looking at him."

Hal struggled to get his breathing under control. "You don't know the truth about the men you aligned yourself with. What they've done to others."

"I'm sure whatever it was they did, it was deserved."

The men behind him growled. But Hal held up a hand to stop them. "Once she's with us, she'll see the truth."

I scoffed. "Don't hold your breath."

Hal held out his hand.

I stared at it for a moment before accepting his shake. I tried to tug my hand back quickly, but Hal held firm.

"What do you think, son? Feel anything?" a deep voice said as a hulking man who resembled a wrestler stepped forward.

"You know, I think I might," Hal said with a sneer.

I jerked my hand free. "There was nothing."

The tall man behind the bond grinned at me. "We'll just see about that."

CHAPTER TWENTY-ONE

Hayden

A CHILL SKITTERED DOWN MY SPINE AT THE MAN'S words. He was older, with gray peppering his hair and beard. But it was the eyes that scared me the most. They were so cold, cruelty swirling in them.

"Now, Dexter. It's not nice to play the big, bad alpha and scare the poor girl," Mona said, slipping her arm through mine.

Alpha. The alpha of the Corbett clan. The one who had called for more than one attack on me and my guys. Anger surged somewhere deep, and I had to fight to choke it down.

Dexter sent Mona a sharkish grin. "Can't help who I am, darlin'."

Mona made a tsking sound as she led me away.

Even as I got some distance from the hordes, nausea rolled through me. Hal was bad, but his father was even worse.

Nolan stepped into our path. "Now, we meet. Alone."

My guys' shifter hearing must've been fully activated because they were on us in a flash.

"You're not taking her *anywhere,*" Cáel growled, his eyes bleeding completely silver.

Nolan seemed unmoved by the display. "How can we trust that Hayden is telling us the truth when you're there *intimidating* her?"

Maddox's eyes swirled with liquid gold. "We don't intimidate innocents. Unlike other people we know."

Nolan stiffened. "Are you making an accusation?"

"You're the one who assumed that," Maddox gritted out.

"Watch yourself, Kavanaugh. You're treading on very thin ice. I'd hate to have to take formal action against you."

Rage blasted out of Maddox. So intense that even I could feel it.

"It's no problem," I said quickly. I would've agreed to stab needles into my eyes if it would've defused the situation. "I'll talk to them and be right back."

"Hayden," Knox said, pain lacing his voice.

I forced a smile. "I'll be fine."

Cillian stepped forward, his massive form menacing. "If you even consider taking Hayden anywhere without her consent, I'll rain hellfire down on you."

Nolan's eyes flashed. "You *dare* to threaten a council member."

"It's not a threat. It's a justified consequence. You're being watched right now. This isn't something you'll be able to cover up as you have in the past."

A muscle in Nolan's jaw twitched, and I knew then that he'd been planning exactly that. I looked at my guys, knowing panic was in my gaze. Cillian squeezed my hand quickly.

"No one's taking you anywhere you don't want to go. There are too many eyes watching," he assured me.

"Let's get this over with already," Arthur muttered from behind Nolan. "I have places to be."

He seemed utterly bored by it all, but Fionn, who stood next to him, was riveted, an interested gleam in his eye.

Mona gave my arm a tug. "This way, Hayden."

I couldn't get a read on her. She didn't seem as evil as Nolan, but if she'd taken money from the hordes to be here tonight, she wasn't exactly noble either.

I glanced over my shoulder, my gaze colliding with Easton's. His hands were clenched at his sides, his jaw tight. With his hair falling around his shoulders, he looked like a warrior from some long-ago world, just dressed in a modern-day suit.

"Good lord, you'll be back with them in a few minutes," Mona muttered. "Get ahold of yourself."

"Going with you all, anything could happen," I shot back.

She chuckled. "Smart girl."

Nolan stormed ahead and down the hallway before ducking into a smaller room that appeared to be a parlor from times past. No one took a seat. The moment Fionn closed the door behind us, Nolan was peppering me with questions.

"Who did you feel a connection with?"

"No one," I said honestly.

He scoffed. "Don't lie to us, girl."

My eyes narrowed on him. "I'm not lying. I know what touching a bond mate feels like. I don't have a connection with any of them."

"That's not what Hal said," Fionn murmured as he took another sip of scotch.

"Well, Hal is a psychopathic liar and an attempted murderer who should have a cactus shoved up his ass, so I'm not surprised," I clipped.

Fionn choked on his drink, beginning to cough.

Nolan glared at me. "The Corbetts are a respected horde that has been around for generations. They are not to be insulted."

"They almost killed me. Twice."

A muscle began fluttering wildly in his jaw. "I'm sure Cillian and his horde started it."

What was this? Kindergarten?

"Can we hurry this up?" Arthur asked, turning to me. "Many of the hordes in that room would offer you your heart's desire. Would you like to entertain offers?"

"No," I answered quickly. "I just want to go home with my bond."

"I'm not sure that horde is a safe place for you," Nolan said smugly. "Not if you've almost been killed *twice*."

Shit. Shit. Shit. Of course, I'd backed myself into a corner. I swallowed hard. "The only reason I'm alive now is because of that horde. They make me feel safe and cared for. I'm not going to trade that for all the jewels and fancy cars and houses in the world."

Fionn tapped a finger against his glass. "Interesting."

Mona sighed. "I really wanted to see what she could get out of them. I do love that game of poker."

Fionn crossed to her, sliding his arm through Mona's. "Why don't you and I head to Monaco after this? I can fuel up the jet, and we can hit the tables."

Mona grinned at him. "I like the way you think."

"Excuse me," Nolan growled. "This is a serious matter."

Mona waved him off. "Give it up, Nols. She wants to stay with her ragtag group. Let her. We got our payouts."

Redness crept up Nolan's throat. "For *now*." And with that, he stalked out of the room.

Fionn sighed. "So dramatic."

Arthur checked his expensive watch. "How much longer do we need to stay?"

Mona flicked her gaze to an antique grandfather clock. "An hour, tops."

Arthur grumbled but headed out the door.

"Shall we return?" Mona asked me.

I swallowed hard. "I'm just going to run to the restroom."

"Of course," she said, tugging Fionn toward the door.

I followed them out, finding a bathroom across the hall. I slipped inside, locking the door behind me. Only then did I begin to tremble. I'd been holding back the fear all night long, but I finally let it flow.

Stumbling back to sit on a bench in the corner, I let my head fall into my hands. Images flashed through my mind of each of the hordes, of the council, but most of all, the Corbetts. The dead look in Hal's eyes, the way Dexter's voice had made my skin crawl.

Pressure built behind my eyes. I just wanted this over with. I wanted to go home.

Home.

The mountain mansion really was starting to feel that way. My safe space with people who made me protected.

Taking a deep breath, I stood. I'd keep fighting these battles. For them.

Smoothing the wrinkles out of my dress, I headed out of the restroom. I hadn't made it two steps before someone shoved me into an alcove.

"Stop playing games, you little bitch."

Hayden

THE ALCOVE HAD SHADOWS SWIRLING AROUND US AS I shoved at the large form's chest.

Dexter Corbett just laughed, low and ugly. "Sorry, *bana-phrionnsa*. You're just a little too tiny."

My knee came up on instinct, thanks to a self-defense class we'd had as part of gym in high school.

But Dexter was too fast. He twisted, avoiding the worst of my hit. I expected rage, maybe even physical violence. But instead, he grinned. That twist of his lips wasn't warm in any way, but there was a hint of grudging respect.

He straightened, taking half a step back. It wasn't enough for me to make a break for it, but it was enough that I could breathe.

Dexter straightened his black suit jacket. "I'll admit, when I saw that you were a tiny wisp of a thing, I didn't think you'd be a fighter."

I simply glared at him. There was nothing I could say that would likely get him to back off. I just needed to bide my time before I could run or someone came to find me.

"I like that you have a bit of fire. It'll serve you well as the alpha female of our horde."

My stomach churned. "I have no interest in being alpha anything, and I certainly don't want a damned thing to do with your horde."

Dexter's eyes narrowed on me. "You're new to this world, Hayden. You'd be wise to watch your step."

I returned his glare, opting for silence once again.

"Cillian and his band of misfits won't be around forever. Legacy and tradition will always find their way back to power."

Something tickled the back of my mind as questions began to form. "And you represent legacy and tradition?"

Dexter straightened. "I come from a long line of royalty. My family has always had ties to leadership, and we always will. People respect that. You should count yourself lucky that my son and his bond have even looked your way."

Nausea hit me in waves. "Your *son* tried to kill me."

Dexter's dark eyes flashed gold. "Easton goaded him into that fight. You never should've gotten in the way. A woman's place is in the home, not in the battle."

I had to swallow back my snort of derision. I was sure Dexter was the type of man who thought women should be barefoot and pregnant in the kitchen. "If your son told you that Easton goaded him, he's flat-out lying. Hal appeared in the alley. He taunted East. And when Easton told him to leave, Hal tried to blast him with fire."

"Lies," Dexter spat.

"Truth," I shot back. "And I will *always* fight for the people I care about. My place is at their side." Not hiding behind them.

Dexter's jaw worked back and forth, but I could see that tiny flicker of doubt about his son's story. *Good.* Maybe I'd make a little trouble for Hal at home.

But the doubt didn't last. Dexter seemed to shake off the possibility of his son's lies and zeroed in on me. "You'll learn your place." That creepy smile stretched across his face again. "You'll make my son an army of dragons, and we'll use them to decimate Cillian and his clan."

My mouth went dry. This was all Dexter and Hal saw women as. Breeders. A means to an end of their battles.

"I'd rather stab myself with a rusty spork, but thanks anyway."

Smoke curled from Dexter's nostrils. "Watch your words, girl."

"I think it's you who needs to watch yourself, Corbett." The smoky voice curled around us, but there was a lethal threat lacing the words.

Dexter whirled to face Maddox. "Maddox," he spat.

"Now, what would the council think if they knew you'd cornered an unprotected female dragon at one of *their* events?" There was a casual air to Maddox's words, but I could feel the anger pulsing beneath them.

Dexter's Adam's apple bobbed as he swallowed. "I was just talking to her."

A muscle beneath Maddox's eye fluttered. "You've got her pinned in a dark corner, towering over her, *threatening* her. I'd hardly call that talking."

Dexter scoffed. "Your word against mine. And I don't think the council listens much to you, Kavanaugh. They never did."

Maddox's hands fisted, his knuckles bleaching white.

Oh, hell.

I shoved past Dexter, grabbing Maddox's wrist and tugging as hard as I could. It was like trying to move a brick wall.

Dexter laughed, low and ugly. "It has to suck, realizing you have no power at all."

A low growl escaped Maddox's throat.

I got right up in his face, making sure it was me who filled his vision. "Mad, *please*. I need to get out of here. Come with me."

It took a moment for him to register me, but then he nodded jerkily, stumbling down the hall.

I kept hold of his wrist, pulling him into another empty room. It wasn't the parlor I'd been in earlier, but it was what looked like a study with one of those antique rolltop desks and Victorian furniture.

Maddox paced the small space, struggling to breathe normally.

I stepped into his path, forcing him toward the small sofa. He stumbled backward, finally sitting. But he wasn't there. Not really. He was a million miles away.

I framed Maddox's face in my hands, forcing his gaze to me. "Come back to me."

Those amber eyes flared, blazing into mine.

"Talk to me," I begged.

Maddox let out a ragged breath. "I want to peel the skin from his body and rip him limb from limb."

Chapter Twenty-Three

Maddox

All I could feel was the fury blazing through me. It blazed through muscle and sinew, leaving behind nothing but ash in its wake. All I could see was Dexter pinning Hayden against the wall. Terrifying her. Telling her all about his *plans* for her future.

But I knew what could happen when the Corbetts got their hands on a female. Knew the agony they could bring.

I rarely let my rage free, but ever since the council had shown their faces at our home, I hadn't been able to rein it in. But maybe the fracturing of my walls had already started. Begun when Hayden had walked unknowingly into our world, blowing everything sky high.

"Mad," she whispered, her voice thick with concern.

Her hands felt like heaven on my cheeks. Her skin was so damned soft. It was unlike anything I'd ever felt before. Because Hayden was *more*.

Even that thought felt like a betrayal. To Niecy. Not because what we'd shared had been some earth-shattering thing, but because of what Niecy had lost. All because of me.

My gut churned, and I pulled back, out of Hayden's touch. Losing that connection felt like a million knives slicing across my skin.

Hurt flashed in Hayden's violet eyes, and I wished those knives were real. She didn't deserve the fucked-up place my head was. The dark demons that lived there. I might've hidden them better than some of my brothers, but that didn't mean they weren't there.

Hayden lowered herself to the tiny ottoman opposite the sofa, not saying a word.

My throat constricted. "Are you all right?" I hadn't even asked if he'd hurt her.

"Physically? I'm fine."

But emotionally, she was anything but. The urge to pull Hayden into my arms was so strong. To cradle her against my chest and let her scent of jasmine and dew fill my nostrils.

My fingers tightened around the edge of the sofa—anything to keep them in check.

"Good."

"But you're not okay," she said softly. "You haven't been."

I saw the hurt in Hayden's expression again, the pain. Emotions that *I'd* put there. But that was what I'd always brought to the people I cared about. Agony.

Hayden pushed on, always my brave Mo Ghràidh. "But it's more than just tonight. You disappeared."

Guilt gnawed at me, digging its claws in and twisting. "I needed to get away for a while."

"To your cabin?"

I tensed. "Who told you about it?"

Hayden didn't pull back as if my harsh tone had hurt her. She studied me as if she was really trying to understand, to *see*. "Is the cabin supposed to be a secret?"

"No," I mumbled. "But not many know about it."

"Knox told me. He knew I was worried about you and wanted me to know you were okay."

Of course, Knox would be concerned about Hayden first and foremost. He'd been all in from the first moment. I envied my brother for how he'd seemed to defeat his demons. He didn't let his past twist him.

I rested my elbows on my knees and braced my head in my hands. "Sometimes all the voices in the house get to be too much. I need quiet. Space." Time to let the rage flow out of me. To shift and fly for hours, burning out the anger.

"What did the council do?" Hayden asked softly.

My head jerked up, tension stringing my muscles taut. I wanted to snap at her, but I couldn't. I'd already caused Hayden too much pain. And maybe if I explained it, she'd see why this could never be. At first, I'd thought it was just fear of losing my job, but it was so much more. Those demons were still haunting me from the deep.

"They didn't do a damned thing when the Corbetts killed Niecy."

Hayden tensed. "Niecy was your...girlfriend?"

I let out a long breath. In for a penny, in for a pound. "Yes. She was my first...everything."

Hayden tried to hide the flicker of hurt, but I didn't miss it.

I didn't know how to explain that there wasn't anything for Hayden to be jealous about. "She was a childhood crush. Those bumbling firsts. But even back then, the Corbetts knew I'd be powerful. They wanted to quelch that."

Hayden's brows pulled together. "You grew up around here?"

I nodded. "A few hours north, almost to Oregon. I was a part of a very small horde. But it was a good one. Niecy was a dragon, but she didn't have the ability to shift. She should've been safe. But not when the Corbetts wanted to send me a message. I was a sophomore at Evergreen when they left her broken body on the hood of my car."

Tears glittered in Hayden's eyes. "I'm so sorry, Maddox."

"I was living the high life in college. I'd turned into a shitty boyfriend. I didn't cheat, but I was so excited to be away from home. There were classes I'd only dreamed of."

Hayden's lips curved the barest amount. "Always the brainiac."

The corner of my mouth kicked up. "From birth, I'm afraid." That smile slipped. "She deserved so much better. We wouldn't have made it to the end of that year, but at least she would've been free to find a mate who loved and cherished her."

"Maddox," Hayden whispered, her voice carrying with it pain that was my own.

My hands fisted. "I didn't know I'd landed on the Corbetts' radar. Not until it was too late."

"And you went to the council to tell them what happened."

"Yes. I smelled the Corbetts' scent all over Niecy's body. But the council said that wasn't proof they were the ones who killed her. She could've been visiting the horde."

"Liars," Hayden gritted out.

"They only care about two things: money and power. It's all they'll ever care about."

She worried her bottom lip. "Was the council made up of the same members as it is now?"

I pulled back, studying her. "No. Nolan is the only member who's the same. Why?"

Hayden gave her head a shake, making her blonde hair cascade over her shoulders. "Nothing." She leaned forward and took my hands in hers. "It wasn't your fault."

I tried to jerk my hands free, but Hayden held firm.

"It wasn't your fault."

"It was," I growled.

Hayden's violet gaze locked with mine. "Maddox, this *wasn't* your fault."

Each word was like a carefully placed blow. And before I knew it, tears were filling my eyes.

Chapter Twenty-Four

Hayden

Maddox's tears were a knife to the heart. This strong, brave man finally breaking under the pressure he'd been under for over a decade. I moved then; I couldn't help it. I climbed onto his lap and wrapped myself around him.

His shoulders shook as he let himself fall apart. Just for a moment. But I didn't let go, even as Maddox struggled to pull himself together.

His face was pressed to the crook of my neck. "Her parents blamed me. It's why I ended up leaving my horde."

I stiffened, my hold on him tightening. I understood that Niecy's parents must've been in the throes of terrible grief, but to place fault on Maddox, who had done nothing wrong? "It was their grief talking. They weren't in their right minds."

"It wouldn't have happened if I hadn't been so hell-bent on going to college."

I pulled back, framing Maddox's face in my hands. "And that

makes you a monster? Wanting to learn? Then I'm a monster, too. Lock me up and stone me."

Maddox glowered. "Don't talk like that."

"Then don't *you* talk about yourself like that either."

His hand lifted, fingers tracing the side of my face. "I'm going to hurt you. I already have."

I steeled myself, staring into those amber eyes that had hypnotized me from the first moment I'd seen them. "Yes. And I'll hurt you. What matters is that we do our best to make it right when it happens."

Maddox shook his head, black hair moving in artful disarray. "It's more, and you know it."

I gripped his face harder, forcing his gaze to mine. "You want to know what hurts the most?"

He stared at me for a long moment. "Yes." The word was barely audible. As if he was terrified to know the answer yet needed it just the same.

"You hiding yourself from me. Not letting me in. I'm not saying that I have a right to all your secrets, but I want to *know* you, Mad. Please."

Under normal circumstances, I would've been embarrassed at my pleading tone. But I was past that. I needed to break down these walls between us, and if begging was what it took, then I'd get down on my knees.

Maddox searched my face, looking for something. "I don't know if I can. It's been a long time since I've let a partner in. I don't know if I'm equipped."

Because if he didn't let his partners truly mean something to him, then they couldn't be a weakness.

My thumbs swept back and forth across his cheeks. "You already are. You did it tonight."

Fear struck through those amber eyes.

"Don't," I whispered. "Don't run from me."

A battle played out across Maddox's expression. "We put you at horrible risk."

"Maybe," I admitted. "But how much more risk would I be at if you *hadn't* found me? What if another horde had? What if the Corbetts had?"

I couldn't help the shiver that ran through me at the thought. I never would've survived their plans for me.

Maddox let out a low growl as his arms came around me, and he crushed me to his chest.

I hated putting those images in his mind, but he needed to know that there were so many worse fates than ending up with five people who cared about me. It might be to varying degrees, but they weren't trying to hurt me or force me to do anything against my will.

Maddox nuzzled my neck. "I need you safe, Mo Ghràidh."

"I am," I whispered.

The door to the study opened, and Nolan strode inside, glaring at us. "There is still an event going on, and Hayden's presence is required."

Another growl built in Maddox's throat. But I squeezed his shoulder hard as I climbed off his lap. "Nolan's right. Let's get the idiot games over with."

"Watch it," Nolan snarled.

Maddox rose, baring his teeth. "As far as I know, speaking the truth isn't a punishable offense. Unless you're planning a military state I don't know about."

Nolan's jaw clenched. "Just get in there."

Without another word, he stormed out.

"Well, that was fun," I mumbled. "His face always looks like he just sat on a porcupine."

Maddox choked on a laugh. "That's certainly an image."

"Poor porcupine."

"Poor porcupine, indeed," Maddox agreed.

As we started for the door, Maddox slid his hand into mine. My gaze jerked up to his face.

He glanced down at me. "I'll mess this up. But if you want, I'll try. I can only be your friend while you're my student. But I'll try."

Hope blazed through my chest, extinguishing the flickers of disappointment at the word *friend*. "I'd like that."

Maddox squeezed my hand and led me down the hall.

The moment we reached the party, we were surrounded by the guys, each of them peppering us with questions. But Cillian was silent, his focus zeroing in on our joined hands. The corners of his mouth tipped up, trying to pull into a smile, but the movement looked rusty.

Maddox glanced over his shoulder, and I followed his line of sight to the Corbetts. Hal was glowering at us while Dexter angrily whispered something into another man's ear.

Maddox turned back to our group. "Dexter cornered Hayden in the hallway."

Low growls and snarls filtered through the air around us. Smoke curled out of Cáel's nostrils, and, as if he couldn't take it anymore, he hauled me against his chest. "Okay. You're okay." He whispered the words over and over again.

My chest squeezed, and I hugged him hard. "I'm fine."

Knox and Easton sent a worried look our way as I pulled Cáel's shirt free and slipped in a hand to give him skin-to-skin contact.

Maddox lowered his voice, pitching it in Cillian's direction. "We're going to have to get creative finding a way home. I'd guess they have traps waiting."

Chapter Twenty-Five

Hayden

We were the first people out the door the moment the cocktail party ended. Instead of the limo waiting, there were three large SUVs. A dozen enforcers milled around the vehicles, scanning the surrounding forests for any sign of attack.

Terry strode forward and handed Cillian a set of keys. "They're in the forest outside our territory."

Cillian let out a low growl. "We won't be able to avoid war for long."

Cáel echoed the sound with one of his own, and his fingers twitched at his sides. He was itching for a fight, to make the Corbetts pay. But the thought of him, of any of them heading into a battle like something out of a vicious fairy tale was more than I could take.

I grabbed Cáel's hand, squeezing it hard.

He looked down at me, emotions warring in his expression.

"We need to move," Maddox said in a low voice.

Knox nodded, opening the door to the back seat and sliding inside. Cáel helped me in after him. I was regretting the choice of dress now. If we were met with trouble, fighting in this thing would be utterly ridiculous. I'd have a boob out in no time. On the upside, maybe flashing my opponent would be a distraction technique.

A laugh bubbled out of me.

Knox's brows pulled together. "Are you okay?"

I nodded, just laughing harder.

Easton's forehead creased as he and Cáel took the seats in front of us. "I think she might be cracking."

Cáel punched him in the chest.

"I'm not saying it to be an asshole. I just meant she's been through a lot over the past few days."

That just made me laugh harder. *A lot* was an understatement. And it was more than the past few days. This last month had been enough to send me into a straitjacket. Meeting five men I was inextricably drawn to. Discovering they were dragon shifters. Discovering that *I* might be one, too. Mates and enemies and the freaking council. I needed a drink, and I wasn't sure there was a strong enough one out there.

Cillian started the engine as Maddox climbed in beside him. "We'll be home soon, but we need to take the long way."

That had the laughter dying on my lips. We needed to take the long way because the Corbetts were waiting on the normal path.

"What if they're this way, too?" I whispered.

Knox pulled me tight against him. "This isn't a route others know about. We have several leading to the property that are hidden."

"Good. That's good." Except I knew they'd created those for a reason. Because this wasn't the first time they'd had trouble. Not the first time they'd been under attack. My stomach twisted in a vicious squeeze.

Cáel looked worried as Cillian pulled away from the house, SUVs full of enforcers flanking us.

"Is this how it always is?" I asked, voice barely audible.

"How what always is?" Knox asked gently.

"Your lives. Someone always out to get you?"

Cillian and Maddox shared a look in the front of the vehicle, and I had my answer.

I had a million other questions on the tip of my tongue, but I swallowed them down. The guys didn't need to be worried about me right now. They needed to focus.

The SUV in front of us picked up speed, and Cillian followed.

Knox held on to me tighter as we took a curve quickly. "It'll be harder for anyone to follow us at this speed. Their tail would be obvious, and the enforcers tailing us would take care of it."

Take care of it. That wasn't exactly accurate. It was more take care of *them*. People, shifters. Yes, they were beings that intended us harm, but it was still taking a life.

A phone rang through the speakers in the SUV. Cillian hit a button on the wheel. "What is it?"

"Single rider. Motorcycle. Hundred yards back," a male voice clipped. "He's riding without his lights, thinking he'll stay out of sight."

"Idiot," Maddox mumbled. "We won't have to kill him. A car will take him out."

"Not taking that chance," Cillian muttered. "Throw the spikes when we hit gravel. Take him alive if you can."

I bit the inside of my cheek so hard I tasted blood.

"Yes, alpha." Then the call cut out.

"They're getting bolder," Easton muttered.

Cillian gripped the wheel harder as we made another sharp turn. "Hayden changed things. They want to get to her before we bond."

My stomach bottomed out. Because they wanted to use me as some fucked-up breeding animal.

Cáel let out a rumbling roar.

The rest of the guys cursed.

His chest rose and fell in ragged pants, and his whole body vibrated. "Need. To. Hunt."

"Control, Cáel," Cillian ordered.

Scales rippled over Cáel's forearms. "Can't."

"Another minute and we'll be in the forest," Knox promised. "Then you can hunt."

Cillian's green gaze flashed in the rearview mirror. "Take him alive."

Cáel growled. "I'll try."

Pain and fear swirled in my chest. "Don't. Stay with us."

Cáel twisted in his seat, agony clear on his face. I wasn't sure if it was from fighting the shift or the fact that he was about to deny me. "I have to, Little One."

We hit gravel, and the SUV slowed. Cáel was out the door with a speed that had his body blurring. A second later, a white-and-silver dragon was taking flight, and the SUV was picking up speed again.

Tears burned the backs of my eyes.

Knox squeezed me tighter. "He needs it, Hayden."

"Why?" I croaked.

"He's been through a lot. If he doesn't let that part out, the part that needs to protect, to hurt those who intend us harm, then there's a chance he could go feral."

I stiffened. "What does that mean?"

Knox and Easton shared a look, but it was Easton who answered. "It means that his human side would lose dominance, and his dragon would take over completely."

"What would his dragon do?" I whispered.

"Hunt. Kill," Easton answered.

Knox looked down at me. "And the Cáel we know would never come back. He'd be in his dragon form forever."

CHAPTER TWENTY-SIX

Hayden

THE THREE SUVs PULLED TO A HALT IN FRONT OF the house, and everyone piled out. My muscles were wound so tightly it was difficult to get them to move. When they finally obeyed, it was in a tripping sort of fall that had me landing with an *oomph* against a hard chest.

Strong hands grabbed my arms. “You okay?”

Easton’s deep rasp swirled around me, and I struggled to straighten. “Sorry, I—”

My words caught in my throat as my gaze met his. I couldn’t help but trace the gold pattern in his green irises. It was so different from Knox’s, but just as hypnotizing.

“Hayden—”

A phone rang out into the quiet night, and Easton dropped his hold on me as if he’d been burned. He took two giant steps back, each one a knife to the chest. I’d thought our talk tonight had brought us closer. Thought it had changed things. But apparently, I was wrong.

“Tell me you got him,” Cillian snarled into a cell phone.

There was silence as we all waited.

The muscles in Cillian's jaw bowed and flexed. "Good. Don't start slicing off fingers until I get there."

I winced at the disgusting image but pushed that aside for more important information. "Was it Cáel? He's okay?"

Cillian jerked his head in a nod. "He's fine. But we need to see what we can get out of the Corbett enforcer."

A wave of nausea rolled through me.

"I'll stay with Hayden," Knox volunteered.

"You don't have to. I'll be okay," I assured them. The truth was, I needed a good cry. The buildup from the past twenty-four hours was too much to take. I needed to let it all go.

"No," Cillian clipped. "One of us needs to stay with you."

I snapped my mouth closed. There'd be no arguing with him in this state. He was too on edge.

Knox wrapped an arm around my shoulders and held me close. "Let's get you inside."

I looked at Cillian, Maddox, and Easton. "Be careful."

There was a cold glint in Maddox's typically warm eyes. "It's not us who needs to worry."

I turned toward the door at that. The past few weeks had already held too much cruelty. I didn't want to think about any more.

Knox led me through the door and into the foyer. "Are you hungry?"

I shook my head. "I just want a shower and bed."

That much was true, but I also needed a little distance from this overload.

"Okay."

Knox guided me up the stairs and toward my bedroom. Once we were inside, I made a beeline for the bathroom, closing the door behind me. I kicked off the too-high heels and unzipped the gorgeous garment. I hung it on the hooks on the door and headed for the massive shower.

It was one of those with a marble bench and too many jets to count. But tonight, I opted for the normal spray. Stepping under the water, I let it course over me.

Memories flashed in my mind. Dexter cornering me. Hal's threats. My fear for Cáel.

A sob tore free. Then another. They tripped over each other in a race for purchase.

My shoulders shook as my tears mixed with the water.

I didn't hear the bathroom door, didn't know a person was even here until the shower door opened. Knox slipped inside, his arms coming around me and holding me to him.

"Let it out. I'm here."

I cried harder, and Knox lowered us to the shower bench, cradling me in his arms as warm water rained over us. He held on and didn't let go. He didn't try to get me to stop or tell me everything would be okay. Because it wasn't. And that was the reality we all had to face.

I wasn't sure how long he held me, but eventually, I had no more tears to cry.

Knox's hand trailed up and down my back in soothing strokes.

"I'm sorry," I croaked.

"There's nothing to be sorry for. Tonight was a lot. You can't bottle up everything that you're feeling."

I pulled back a fraction. "I don't see how it's possible for this to work. It feels like the whole world is against us."

Knox's hand moved to my neck, kneading the muscles there. "I won't lie to you. We'll have to deal with the Corbetts. They won't stand for us having a mate."

"Why do they care so much?"

Knox's mouth curved. "Sometimes I forget that you didn't grow up in this world. Being mated will make all of us stronger, faster, our abilities heightened."

My mouth went slack. "Oh."

"They don't want that for us, but more, they want it for themselves."

My stomach cramped at the thought.

Knox squeezed my neck. "We'll deal with them. And once we're mated, things will ease a bit."

But I wasn't sure we'd ever get there. Not anytime soon. Maddox may have softened to me tonight, but he was firm in not touching me until I graduated. And Easton…he wasn't any closer to letting me in, even if he'd stopped with his assholish ways.

My gaze lifted to Knox's. "Make me forget? Just for tonight?"

His eyes flared. "Hayden…"

"Please." I wasn't above begging.

Knox searched my face, looking for something. He must've found it because he took my mouth then. The kiss was different. It was slow and tender. It poured emotion into me that made my eyes sting.

His hand moved to my breast, palming it and squeezing gently. His thumb circled my nipple, and it beaded under his touch.

Knox pulled his mouth from mine, breathing just a little more raggedly. "I could drown in your taste."

My core tightened, spasming around nothing but the need for him.

I moved then, straddling Knox's lap and resting my hands on his shoulders. He gazed up at me, reverence in his eyes.

"So damn beautiful." His hand dipped between my thighs, teasing, toying.

"I want all of you," I whispered.

Gold sparked in Knox's eyes as two fingers slid inside me. "Are you sure?"

"Never been surer of anything." I needed to be as close as possible to this man who had cared for me before he'd even known who I was to him. This man who had shown me kindness before knowing I was anything but a bumbling freshman, lost on her way to check-in.

His fingers stretched me, and I couldn't hold in my moan.

"I've wanted you since the moment I saw you. When I thought you were a human and knew I shouldn't go anywhere near you."

My eyes locked with his. "You made me feel safe from the moment I met you. You made me feel special. And you showed me true kindness."

Knox's free hand lifted to my face, cupping it. "I love you, Hayden. You saw me, even the things I tried to hide."

Pressure built behind my eyes. "I love you, too. More than I thought possible."

Then Knox's fingers were gone, and I was sliding down onto him. My eyes watered with the stretch, my mouth falling open.

"Breathe, beautiful. Just breathe. You were meant to take me," Knox whispered.

His fingers twisted my nipple, making my core spasm, and he cursed.

"Gonna kill me," he muttered.

"That was all your doing."

Knox nipped my bottom lip, then kissed me hard and needy.

Everything went to liquid heat inside me. I rocked my hips, the friction sending delicious shivers through me.

Knox moaned into my mouth, his hips rising to meet mine.

I pulled back. "More," I pleaded.

Then he really started to move. He thrust deep, one arm holding me in place. The angle had him hitting my G-spot over and over. Each contact had tears spilling free.

"Knox," I moaned.

"Meant for me," he growled. "Meant to take my cock. Meant to be mine."

My inner walls trembled at his words.

The action sent him into a frenzy. He pushed up from the bench, bracing my back against the wall as he slammed into me. The sheer force had my orgasm hitting with the force of a freight train.

I cried out in some nonsensical words, my nails digging into his shoulders.

Knox roared as he came, emptying into me. The feel of his cum inside me had a fresh orgasm hitting me, milking him for everything he had to give. And then I passed right out.

Chapter Twenty-Seven

Cael

"Don't get blood on the fucking rugs," Cillian snapped as he stepped through the front door.

I just snarled in his direction.

Maddox shook his head. "They *are* handmade from Egypt."

Easton snorted as he brought up the rear.

I tried to find humor in Maddox trying to lighten the mood, but I couldn't. My beast was still riding me hard. The enforcer's blood wasn't enough for him. He wanted more.

Footsteps sounded on the stairs, and we looked up to find Knox striding down them.

"Where's Hayden?" Cillian asked instantly.

"Asleep." His gaze moved to me. "Holy shit. Did someone go *Carrie* on your ass?"

I glowered at him. So, I might've had a little blood on me. So what? "I never knew you assholes were so sensitive."

"Get changed," Cillian growled. "Then we'll talk."

My back teeth ground together, but I jogged up the stairs, Knox giving me a wide berth. The pull to go to Hayden's side of the floor was strong, but I knew if I peeked in on her now, I'd never leave. My dragon held too much of the reins.

Instead, I forced myself to head in the direction of my bedroom. I flicked on the light. The blue on the walls was meant to be calming, but it didn't do a damned thing to soothe my beast right now.

I moved to the bathroom, turning on the light there, too. As I did, I took in my reflection and winced. Maybe my brothers had a point. I might've gone a bit overboard in our session with the enforcer.

My dress shirt was plastered to my chest with blood. There was spray across my face and in my hair. Thank the gods I'd taken my favorite leather jacket off before I'd gotten to work.

I shucked my clothes and tossed them in the garbage. Taking the fastest shower known to man, I donned sweats and a tee. I was itchy. My dragon wanted to hunt again. Or fuck. But mostly, he wanted to claim Hayden. But if I let him at her now, he'd scare the shit out of her.

I forced myself to head for the kitchen, where I knew my brothers would be. It was our favored late-night meeting spot. One where Knox could easily snack, and there was whiskey on hand for Cillian. When I stepped into the massive space, all talking ceased.

"You look remarkably less like a serial killer," Easton muttered.

I bared my teeth at him. "I could change that if you want."

"Enough," Cillian said, exhaustion in his voice.

Guilt gnawed at me. I didn't want to make things harder for Cill. He had enough on his shoulders. I slid onto an empty stool at the kitchen island and glanced at Knox. "How was she?"

A shadow passed over his features. "Tonight was too much for her. She had a bit of a breakdown."

I stiffened, a fresh wave of anger sweeping through me. I wanted to gut that enforcer all over again. But more than that, I wanted to hunt Hal and Dexter and leave their body parts littered across their territory as a warning.

"How bad?" Maddox asked, his finger tightening on a mug of tea.

"Could've been a lot worse. She's strong. She had a hard cry, and then…" Knox's words trailed off.

"And then you fucked her," Easton finished for him.

Knox moved to deck his twin, but Easton knew the move was coming and evaded it. "Am I wrong?"

"It wasn't like that," Knox growled. "She said she needed me."

Cillian held up a hand. "She's our mate. She'll need physical closeness in times of stress."

My back teeth ground together. I didn't begrudge Knox for being there for Hayden when she needed him, but my beast wanted the same.

"What'd you find out from the enforcer?" Knox asked, clearly ready to change the subject.

Cillian cracked his neck. "Not a whole hell of a lot."

Maddox took a sip of tea. "The Corbetts must do desensitization training."

I grunted in agreement. The enforcer hadn't broken until all his fingers and half of his toes were gone.

"We didn't learn anything we didn't already know," Cillian said. "They want Hayden, and he said they won't stop until they have her."

My beast roared, pushing against my skin. I gripped the edge of my stool, letting the metal bite into my palms.

A muscle under Knox's eye fluttered. "Did he share their plans about how they were going to attempt that?"

Cillian shook his head. "He didn't know."

"How can you be sure?" Knox pressed.

"Because he still wouldn't tell us when Cáel had his intestines wrapped around his fist," Easton mumbled.

Knox's shoulders fell. "Shit."

"For now, the plan is the same. We stick close to Hayden. We double her enforcer detail. Nowhere alone," Cillian ordered.

"We need to bond," Knox said.

The room went wired.

"I *can't*," Maddox said. "Not until she's no longer a student. If we mate, my dragon won't be able to keep from touching her at school."

Knox glared at him. "Then maybe you need to switch jobs. This is more important."

Maddox opened his mouth to argue, but Cillian held up a hand to stop him. "We can't force this on Hayden. She needs time to make this choice. As much as most of us want this, we can't rush her."

He glanced at Easton, who slid off his stool. "I need to call it a night. Early class tomorrow."

Knox watched his brother haul ass out of the kitchen. "This is such a clusterfuck. She needs us."

Just the words had my dragon surging to the surface again. I stood, heading for the door. "I need to get some sleep, too."

It was a lie.

I needed to see Hayden. To feel her body curled against mine. To rest my hand over her heart and feel it beat beneath my palm.

I was out the door before anyone could say a word. Jogging up the stairs, I headed for her room. I didn't turn on any lights as I slipped inside, letting my vision adjust to the darkness. But the moment I did, I heard a whimper.

My body reacted before my brain, striding toward the huge bed in the center of the room.

Hayden made another sound of distress, a cry almost.

I sank to the mattress, my hand going to her face. "Little One."

She batted at my arm, jerking upright, her eyes going wide.

The moment she registered it was me, she threw herself at my chest.

I caught her, my arms wrapping around her small form. "It's okay. It was just a bad dream. I'm here."

Hayden trembled against me. "It wasn't a dream."

I pulled back, taking her in. "It wasn't?"

She shook her head, blonde hair flying around her. "It was a memory." She took a shaky breath. "I think Dexter Corbett killed my parents."

Hayden

Four sets of angry eyes looked back at me. I was sure Cáel's were angry, too. I just couldn't see them because he hadn't let me go since my nightmare. Even now, I was cradled in his lap on my bed while the rest of the guys paced my bedroom.

"One more time," Cillian ordered.

I let out a shaky breath. "The men that came that night. They spoke a different language. But it sounds like what you guys sometimes speak."

"Gaelic," Maddox offered, his voice the mask of calm.

I nodded. "The main man kept asking where *she* was, but he used another word, too. In that language. Bonna-free-en-sa?"

The guys shared a look.

"*Bana-phrionnsa*?" Maddox asked.

I nodded.

Knox scrubbed a hand over his cheek. "It's a term of endearment a lot of men use." He glanced at me. "Could whoever it was have been Hayden's birth father or an uncle? Even a grandfather?"

My stomach churned at the suggestion. Could my mother have been running from an abusive relationship or abusive family and that was why she was killed? I shivered, and Cáel gripped me harder.

Knox saw the action and instantly moved to the bed, kicking off his shoes and climbing on top of the mattress. He took my legs, laying them over his lap and framing my face in his hands. "Whatever it is, we're going to keep you safe."

"It sounded like him," I said softly. "It sounded like Dexter."

Maddox cleared his throat. "It's completely natural that your subconscious would give the attacker Dexter's voice."

I frowned at Maddox, but he kept going.

"Your brain is reprocessing trauma from your past in a new light now that you know you're a shifter. Compound that with Dexter's threats tonight and you get a nightmare like the one you had."

I shivered again at the memory of it. The nightmare wasn't exactly a true memory. I heard the voices as they'd been all those years ago, but then one of them found me in the attic and pulled me down. And it was Dexter who was looming over me.

I bit my bottom lip, worrying it between my teeth. "Maybe."

But the more that I thought about it, the more I could hear the similarities in the tones.

"Many dragons come from Irish ancestry and speak Gaelic," Knox explained. "It's not uncommon for our kind to have those roots."

"Either way, we're going to be looking into who hurt your parents," Cillian promised.

I swallowed hard. "Thank you."

He jerked his head in a nod as a look of longing swept over his face. "We'll start on it tonight."

It felt like it had been ages since Cillian had held me, and maybe that was what the look of longing was now. It was as if I could never get enough touch from any of them, my body craving it more and more. I was guessing it had something to do with the mate bond. Even though we hadn't cemented it with those bites, I could feel it growing.

"Do you need me?" Knox asked. "I was going to stay up here."

Cillian shook his head. "You and Cáel stay with Hayden."

My body relaxed into Cáel at that. It might've made me a wimp, but I didn't want to be alone.

Cillian's gaze locked with me, those irises going from green to black. "I'm sorry Dexter scared you tonight. He won't get the chance to do it again."

Fury made Cillian's voice vibrate with each word.

"I'm okay," I promised.

"You're not," he gritted out. "But you will be."

With that, he stormed out of the room.

Maddox gave me one last look and then followed after him. Easton didn't look at me at all.

I burrowed into Cáel's chest as Knox massaged one of my feet. I didn't have the energy to try to decipher those two. I was so tired my bones ached.

Knox's thumbs dug into the arch of my foot. "I'm sorry I wasn't here when you had the nightmare. I shouldn't have left you."

"It's not your fault. I'm going to have to be alone now and then."

Cáel grunted in disagreement.

I pinched his side. "If you try to come to the bathroom with me, we're going to have problems, mister."

Knox chuckled at that. "He might try."

Cáel grumbled something indiscernible under his breath.

Knox's green-gold gaze lifted to mine. "No sleeping alone for a while, though. That okay with you?"

"Yeah," I whispered. I never felt safer than when one of them was surrounding me as I slept. Even better if it was more than one. No nightmares would reach me then.

Càit a bheil a' bhana-phrionnsa??

The deep tenor rang out in my head, casting a fresh tremor through me and finally giving voice to my fear. "What if it was Dexter who killed my parents? What if he was looking for me?"

Knox's ministrations stilled, and Cáel gripped me tighter. He let out that rumbling growl in my ear. "Then I'll end him. And I won't spare him an ounce of pain when I do."

Chapter Twenty-Nine

Cillian

I paced the length of my office. It had always felt large and spacious, the massive windows looking out onto the forest making me feel at one with nature. But not tonight. Tonight, it felt as if the walls were closing in.

"Breathe, Cill," Maddox urged.

I knew my eyes flashed black as I whirled on him. "Breathe?" I growled.

Easton winced. "Bad move, Mad."

But Maddox stood his ground. "We're not going to be able to do a damned thing if you're two seconds away from shifting."

"Corbett scared her so badly she had a fucking nightmare. She'd been *crying*."

Just the thought of the tear tracks on Hayden's face had me wanting to tear the entire house down. To shift and fly to Corbett territory and take Dexter on right now.

Maddox's eyes swirled with molten gold. "I *know*. You think I don't want to remove his still-beating heart from his body?"

Somehow, Maddox's anger soothed my own. Just the knowledge that he was as enraged as I was. That he *cared.*

I let out a long breath and collapsed back into my desk chair, pinching the bridge of my nose. I didn't want to send my people to war. Especially not when the Corbetts had greater numbers than we did. No matter how things went, lives would be lost.

Maddox and Easton sat in the chairs opposite my desk, eyeing me carefully.

"They aren't going to let this go," I said finally.

"No, they aren't," Maddox finally agreed.

Easton's jaw clenched. "It's time to eliminate them for good. The Corbetts have brought nothing but pain to the supernatural community. Others would join with us."

He had a point there. I was sure we could find other clans to aid us in battle. But it didn't change the fact that lives would be lost. "And would you be okay if one of us died in that war?"

This time it was Easton's eyes that flashed gold. "They won't get the better of us."

"But they'll get the better of *someone*. A being who is someone's sister, brother, mother, father, child. A being that is someone's whole world. We need to know that there is no other option before we go there." My tone wasn't harsh, but the words still had Easton ducking his head.

Maddox drummed his fingers along his thigh. "It's possible that if we eliminated their leadership, things could change."

I leaned back in my chair. "It's not a bad idea. We'd need Dexter, Hal, their head enforcer…"

"Sean Corbett is one of the other higher-up enforcers. If we could put him in the position to seize power, things might change. He doesn't like the way his uncle leads the horde. That's plain as day," Maddox suggested.

Easton nodded in agreement. "I know there are others who don't agree with his leadership. They just don't hold power."

God, I hoped I was never like that asshole. That the people in my horde always felt like they had a voice. That they felt like I protected them. And part of that protection meant doing everything I could to avoid war.

"Draw up some plan options," I told Maddox. "Different ways to execute. We'll need to take them all at once. If we don't, we risk retaliation. We can't have any witnesses."

Maddox lifted his chin in assent. "I'll get to work on it first thing tomorrow morning."

"What about looking into Hayden's parents' death?" Easton asked.

I sighed. "I've put out feelers about her, and so far, nothing."

Maddox shifted in his seat. "Did you talk to your brothers?"

He still wasn't used to using the term when it came to me. I'd been sure my half brothers wouldn't have wanted a damn thing to do with a bastard brother who would throw into question their right to a crown. But they hadn't given a damn about any crown. They'd just wanted help in taking down our evil father. And that I'd been happy to do.

"Neither Dec nor Ronan has been able to find out anything about Hayden or her parents," I admitted. "But I'm guessing her parents were living under false identities."

I had a number of contacts, many of them comfortable using less-than-legal means, but they still had come back empty-handed.

Easton glanced away.

"What?" I prodded, instantly sensing *something*.

He worried the inside of his cheek. "You could reach out to the Diablos pack."

Just the name had my spine stiffening.

"Are you insane?" Maddox snapped. "You want to ask those psychos for *help*?"

Easton shrugged. "Supposedly, they can find *anyone*."

"Yeah, for the price of your soul," Maddox muttered.

I'd heard the rumors about the Diablos pack. They were mercenaries in our world. Working in the shadows.

Maddox stared at me. "You aren't seriously considering this?"

I scrubbed a hand over my stubbled jaw. "My typical resources are coming up empty."

"And what happens when they get a sniff of Hayden? Decide they'd get a better price for her?" Maddox snarled.

"She's an innocent," I argued.

It was said that the Diablos pack had a code. No harm could come to innocents at their hands. The problem was, me and my brothers were far from innocent. So, while they might not harm Hayden, there were no promises that the same would be true for the rest of us.

"Fucking feral wolves," Maddox muttered.

Easton's lips twitched. "I don't know, man. I'd be kind of curious to meet them."

I studied Maddox for a moment. "Do you think there's any chance Hayden's dream was actually a memory? That Dexter was the one to kill her parents?"

If that were true, there was truly no prayer of him giving up on her.

Maddox pinched the bridge of his nose. "What I said upstairs is true. Her brain is trying to make sense of various traumas. It could easily place Dexter as the villain because of tonight. Or..."

"Dexter could've been after Hayden since she was eleven," I gritted out.

Maddox nodded grimly.

I pulled my cell out of my pocket. "I'm calling the Diablos pack."

Either way, we needed to know who was after Hayden. Even if it meant selling our souls to the devil.

Chapter Thirty

Hayden

I blinked against the thick fog of sleep. I felt like I'd taken a double dose of NyQuil or something. Bright light streamed in through the massive windows. I frowned. Too bright.

Glancing at the clock on the side of the bed, I jerked upright.

"Whoa," Knox said, his hand coming down to steady me. "Are you okay? Another nightmare?"

Worry creased his brow, but I was too concerned with the fact that he was fully dressed to be slowed by that. I threw off the covers and hopped out of bed. "Why didn't you wake me? I already missed my first class, and I'm going to be late for my study session with Wren."

Knox followed me into the bathroom. "You needed sleep."

I glared at him as I shoved my toothbrush into my mouth. "That's not for you to decide," I mumbled as I pulled out the toothbrush. I'd set my alarm last night, but I wasn't surprised that Knox had turned it off. That interfering, overprotective dragon.

I hurried through brushing my teeth and washing my face as Knox looked on.

"You need to take care of yourself," he argued.

"You're right, I do. But part of that is staying on top of my studies," I shot back as I hurried toward the closet.

"What's going on?" Cáel asked as he strode into the bedroom.

"Hayden's pissed we turned off her alarm."

I shot Cáel a glare. "You were in on it, too?"

He winced and glanced at Knox. "Thanks for throwing me under the bus."

"It was your idea," Knox groused.

I ignored them both and hurried to the stack of jeans in the closet. I pulled out a pair and then found a T-shirt and sweater to pair with them. I shucked my pajamas, not caring they were both in the closet.

Low, rumbling growls filled the air.

I held up a hand as I grabbed underwear and a bra from a drawer. "Don't even think about it. I'm late enough already."

Knox tried to move into my space. "I could make being later so totally worth it."

"Keep your distance, green eyes," I clipped, but heat pooled low in my belly. Damn them both.

I pulled on my clothes as quickly as possible.

"I hate school," Cáel muttered.

Knox chuckled. "Definitely seeing the perks of graduating early."

"Men," I huffed, heading out of the closet and grabbing my backpack.

I didn't wait for them. If they weren't ready to leave, I'd just ask one of the enforcers to take me to campus.

"Wait up," Knox called.

"You're too slow," I yelled back.

"I'm trying to get my hard-on under control, thanks to that ass shot."

I choked on a laugh as I nearly ran into a tall form. I skidded to a stop, gazing up into green-gold eyes.

"Ass shot, huh?" Easton asked.

I licked my lips. "It, uh, wasn't my fault. They made me late."

Knox and Cáel came thundering down the stairs.

"You ready, East?" Knox asked.

He nodded and then handed me a cup and a bag.

I took them slowly, staring down at them. "What is it?"

"Hot chocolate and a chocolate croissant," he answered gruffly.

I looked up at him. "Is it poisoned?"

Easton rolled his eyes as he turned for the door. "Shut up."

My mouth curved. "Thank you, Grumpy Cat."

He flipped me his middle finger, and I laughed. But warmth filled me at the idea that Easton had brought me something, but more than that, he'd paid attention to what I liked.

"These lab write-ups," I muttered as my fingers flew across the keyboard. I loved the actual science, but having to give voice to our findings took for-freaking-ever.

Wren looked up from her notes, lips twitching. "Well, we did get a little behind."

I winced. "I'm so sorry you got a dud for a lab partner."

She shook her head. "You're not a dud. But you have had a hell of a start to the school year."

Understatement of the century. Thankfully, Maddox had given us a generous extension on our lab work. But I wanted to get it done.

"I'm really hoping for boring for the rest of the semester." But somehow, I doubted that would happen.

Wren glanced to the table a few over from us where Cáel, Easton, and Knox sat working on their own schoolwork. And I knew Pete and Terry were patrolling the library. "How are you doing?"

I shifted in my seat. It had only been a few hours since Knox and Cáel had kissed me goodbye, but I was starting to get twitchy. Like a foreign energy was humming beneath my skin. "I'm good. Still recovering a bit, but mostly good."

That was the normal thing to say, right? People thought I'd been shot. When in reality, the injury from that blast of dragon fire I'd taken had completely healed, leaving only a faint scar behind.

Wren worried her bottom lip. "If you ever need anything, I'm always here."

I studied her for a moment. Her dark brown hair acted as a sort of shield from the world. But her piercing blue eyes locked with mine, and I knew she meant it. "Thank you."

"Here you go, ladies," Knox said, depositing two sodas and some vending machine snacks on the table. "Thought you might need some study sustenance."

He bent then, slipping a hand under my hair and pressing his lips to my temple. The moment his skin brushed mine, that phantom energy eased, and I could breathe again.

I grabbed his arm, pulling Knox down for a kiss. "Thank you," I whispered.

His mouth curved against mine. "Anything you need. Always."

And I knew Knox meant it.

He released me slowly, and I knew it was hard for him to walk away. But I didn't mind watching his ass as he went.

Wren cleared her throat, and my gaze snapped to her.

"Knox..." she whispered. "He treats you okay? His, uh, friends, too?"

Wren's voice was barely audible, but I frowned.

"He treats me amazingly. They all do. Honestly, I've never had people who cared for me so much."

All the tension went out of Wren on an exhale. "Good. That's good."

My frown deepened as I watched her, but her focus dropped to her textbook. "It's not always like that."

Chapter Thirty-One

Hayden

My bare feet padded down the carpeted hall toward my bedroom. Cáel poked his head out of the door. "Ready for bed?" His lips twitched. "I like the atom pajamas."

My cheeks heated. The guys had clearly told Sharee some of my favorite things, and she'd worked that into my wardrobe. "I was just looking for Cillian."

He'd been MIA all day, and it was starting to feel like it had been years since I'd even had a hug from him.

Knox strode up behind Cáel, and they shared a look.

I stiffened. "Where is he?"

Neither of their expressions spoke of anything good, and that had anxiety racing through me.

"He's fine," Knox assured me. "Just on horde business. Mad is with him."

A little of my tension eased at that. I knew Maddox would have Cillian's back through anything and vice versa. I bit my bottom lip. "Is it about me?"

Cáel frowned, tugging me to him. He rubbed the spot between my eyebrows. "Don't like when you have worry lines."

I nuzzled into him. "Then maybe you guys shouldn't make me worry."

Knox chuckled at that. "Don't hold your breath on that one. But for now, you need sleep."

I didn't miss how they'd avoided my question. But that itself was an answer. I sighed, and Cáel lifted me into his arms. I didn't fight him on it. I was too tired.

I could tell I was still getting my energy back from my injuries. I mostly felt back to normal, but at the end of a long day like this one, fatigue won out.

Cáel laid me gently in the center of my massive bed, and I crawled under the covers. I pinned him with my most intimidating stare. "Turn on my alarm, please."

One corner of his mouth kicked up, but he hit a button on my clock.

"Thank you." I dropped back onto the pillows.

Cáel reached behind his head and tugged off his tee. Shucking his gray sweats, he was left in nothing but black boxer briefs.

My eyes roamed over him. His entire form was decorated with intricate artwork. I really studied the skull covering his chest. In each eye socket was a landscape with mountains and a starry sky. In the sky were dragons.

"You keep staring at me like that and you won't get the sleep you need," Cáel said huskily.

Suddenly, sleep was the last thing on my mind.

Knox climbed into bed behind me, pulling me against his naked form. "We all need sleep."

"Then you probably should've worn some pajamas to bed," I huffed.

He chuckled. "Close your eyes."

Cáel slid into bed on my other side, brushing his lips against mine as he turned out the light. "Good night, Little One."

"Good night," I whispered.

I didn't think sleep would find me easily, but it quickly pulled me under. Only it was far from peaceful.

Branches slapped at my arms and face. The cuts and scratches stung as I ran faster, pushing my muscles as hard as I could go.

"Càit a bheil a' bhana-phrionnsa??" a deep voice bellowed behind me.

Terror shot through me. I knew the owner of the voice. Knew he was the one who had killed my mother.

I pushed myself harder, my lungs seizing. My foot caught on a root, and I hit the ground hard. I struggled to get up, but it was too late.

"There she is. My bana-phrionnsa," the man growled.

I struggled to roll over, to ready myself for defense. And when I did, I saw the owner of the voice.

Dexter Corbett.

I jerked upright, breathing hard. My pajamas, damp with sweat, clung to my body.

Knox was sitting up in a flash. "Hayden. Are you okay?"

I shook my head. "It was another dream. Dexter again."

Cáel hauled me against him. "You're safe."

I let the beat of his heart soothe my frayed nerves. "It was so real," I whispered.

Knox rubbed a hand up and down my arm, sharing a look with Cáel.

Cáel brushed his lips across my hair. "They'll fade with time. I promise."

"How do you know?" I croaked.

He was quiet for a moment. "Because I used to have them."

"More like night terrors," Knox said softly.

I felt Cáel wince.

"They were bad," he muttered.

I pulled back, twisting so that I could see Cáel's face. "From what happened when you were younger?"

He nodded jerkily, swallowing hard. "I showed signs of being a strong shifter early. My alpha used to brag about what a great warrior I'd be. Word spread."

My stomach knotted, dread seeping in.

"Another horde decided they wanted to use me for themselves. They kidnapped me when I was thirteen. Tortured me to try to break me so that they could get allegiance to their horde."

Knox muttered a series of curses about the horde.

I pressed my face to Cáel's neck, and for the first time, I felt the scars there. Mottled skin he'd covered with ink. "I'm so sorry," I whispered, tears clogging my throat, the wetness slipping out and dampening Cáel's flesh. As if those tears could take it all away.

"Don't cry, Little One." Cáel stroked my face. "I got out."

"How?"

"My dragon gave me the strength. He went feral inside me, and I broke the bindings. I killed the guards in the cabin, then slaughtered each and every one of those that had held me."

I shivered in Cáel's hold. "I'm glad."

He pressed his forehead to mine. "I'm not a good man, Hayden."

"Yes, you are. One of the best I've ever known," I whispered.

"She's right," Knox croaked. "You could've killed the whole horde. But you held your dragon back. You only ended those who hurt you."

Cáel's eyes bled to silver. "You guys saved me."

I looked up at him in question.

"I was a lone dragon, couldn't stand being with other people, even shifters. But I got into a jam with some vampires. Cillian saved my ass." Cáel looked at Knox. "And the rest of them. They made me feel like I belonged, like I had a family again."

Knox reached out slowly, making it clear he was going to touch Cáel and giving him all the time in the world to pull away. But Cáel didn't, and Knox's hand came down on Cáel's shoulder. "You're our family. And you make us so much better."

Tears burned the backs of my eyes as my gaze moved between

the two of them. A certainty flew through me. "Make me yours. Fully yours. And everything that comes with it. I want to be your mate."

Knox sucked in a breath. "Hayden…"

"I'm sure," I cut him off.

Cáel let out a low growl.

My hands lifted to both their faces. "Please. I need you. Both of you."

Hayden

Knox's hand tangled in my hair. "This isn't something you can undo, Hayden. This is forever, and we live a hell of a long time."

"I know," I whispered. "Hearing Cáel's story, what he went through, I realized something."

Cáel's light blue eyes were still swirling silver as he gazed down at me.

"We were meant for each other. All the pain, all the scars, we were meant to help each other heal. To keep each other safe. To love each other. And I love you. Both of you. Nothing is ever going to change that. I want to feel what it's like to be connected with you in every way."

Cáel's breaths came faster and faster. "Little One, my dragon is damaged. He is going to be insanely possessive of you once we're mated."

My lips twitched. "Like he isn't already?"

Knox choked on a laugh. "She has a point there."

Cáel's hand ghosted over my cheek. "I want to know you're sure."

I leaned into him, brushing my lips against his. "I've never been more sure of anything."

Knox's hands moved to my pajama top, ripping it open in one swift movement. Buttons flew across the room.

Cáel growled as he took in my bare breasts. His tattooed hands lifted to palm them. "So soft. So perfect."

"Just like all of you," Knox murmured against my neck. He licked and sucked, nipping occasionally.

I pressed my thighs together, need already pulsing there.

Knox's hands traced down my sides, and then claws lengthened from his fingertips. The feel of them against me made me shiver. Then they were slicing down the legs of my pajamas.

"Those were my favorite," I grumbled. But that grumble quickly turned into a moan as Cáel's lips closed around my nipple.

I straddled his lap, giving him better access. "Cáel," I breathed.

His teeth grazed the peak, and I shuddered against him, feeling his cock harden against me.

Then Knox was there, pressing in behind me. His arm circled me, hand dipping between my legs.

I pressed up on my knees in answer, giving him purchase.

"So wet," Knox muttered against my neck, and then two fingers slid inside.

I tipped my head back, leaning on Knox's shoulder and letting out a mewling sound.

Cáel sucked my nipple harder.

"Are you sure you're ready, Hayden? Ready to take us both at once?" Knox crooned.

A shiver raced through me. "At once?" I panted.

He nipped my neck as his fingers slid out of me. "Here and"—they moved between my ass cheeks—"here."

My mouth fell open.

"You were made for it," Knox whispered. "It's typical for

shifters to take their partners at once. Your body will adjust. Your tight little hole will milk my cock while your pussy strangles the life out of Cáel's." He took the wetness from his fingers, spreading it over his dick.

"Oh, God," I mumbled as his finger pressed in. My core convulsed, needing so desperately to be filled.

Cáel released his hold on my nipple and jerked his boxer briefs down. He stroked himself once, twice. A bead of pre-cum leaked from his tip. I wanted that inside me. All of him inside.

Cáel's eyes locked with mine. "Take me, Little One. Take all of me."

It was all I needed. I moved then, balancing my hands on the headboard and slowly lowering myself onto Cáel. My mouth fell open at the brutal stretch, nonsensical sounds leaving my lips.

"You look so beautiful taking his cock, Hayden. Letting it stretch you," Knox crooned as he traced a finger down my spine.

My core tightened at his praise, making Cáel let out a growl. He gripped my chin, yanking my face to his and plundering my mouth. I moaned, making Cáel's dick twitch inside me.

Knox's finger slid between my ass cheeks again, circling that hole.

Heat sparked and danced as I rocked against Cáel in testing thrusts. His fingers closed around my hips in a bruising grip. He met me in finding our tempo. Each arc of his hips sent a kaleidoscope of colors dancing in front of my vision.

Knox moved in behind me, straddling Cáel's legs. The tip of his cock nestled between my ass cheeks. "Tell me you're ready."

"I'm ready," I breathed.

As Cáel withdrew, Knox pressed in. So slowly it was almost painful. A cry left my lips.

"Never seen anything more beautiful," Cáel whispered.

Knox wrapped my hair around his fist, his other hand on the headboard. "You're heaven and hellish torture."

As Knox retreated, Cáel thrust in.

The warring sensations were almost more than I could handle. They picked up speed, battling for dominance. It was as if Cáel and Knox were speaking into each other's minds, driving me to the point of breaking. But I couldn't wait to shatter.

"Can't hold on," Knox bit out.

Cáel growled, his teeth lengthening.

"Now!" Knox commanded.

They both thrust inside me. So full. So tight. So them. As they released, they both bit down on opposite shoulders.

I cried out as pleasure unlike I'd ever known coursed through me. Pleasure and feral need as their release pulsed inside me. I wanted it all and more. A red haze filled my vision and along with it a need to bite. To mark. To make them both mine in every way.

As their teeth retracted from my skin, I moved on instinct. I flew forward, teeth sinking into Cáel's pec. He howled in pleasure, thrusting even deeper inside me. Something crackled in my brain. A rightness. A completion.

Mate.

I released my hold on Cáel and twisted, biting down on Knox's bicep. His hold on my hair tightened as he arched into me. "Mine," he snarled.

And I felt the same. A fresh wave of sensation coursed through me. A belonging. A possession.

They were mine, and I was theirs. And I would fight to the death to protect that.

Chapter Thirty-Three

Hayden

A comforting heat wrapped around me like a cocoon. I let out a little moan as I burrowed deeper into it. A body pressed against me from behind, and another nuzzled my neck from the front.

Everything about the moment was pure bliss. I was happier than I could ever remember being, and it was then that I realized I wasn't just feeling my own joy. I was feeling others'.

The emotions were like colors, each one carrying a different hue. Knox's had a giddiness to it. As if he couldn't believe that we had found each other and managed to cement the bond. Cáel's had a grounded peacefulness. As if he was at ease for the first time since his attack.

And I could feel those emotions pouring into me and through me.

My eyes popped open, and Cáel pulled back, taking me in. "How do you feel?"

My mouth opened and closed a few times before I could get [illegible]

Knox hardened against my backside. "Don't go saying that first thing. I already have morning wood."

A laugh bubbled out of me, and I smacked his arm. "I meant your emotions. I can feel how happy you are."

Knox brushed my hair out of the way and pressed a kiss to his claiming mark. A heated shiver wracked my body.

"Never been so happy," he whispered hoarsely.

"Me neither."

I lifted a hand to Cáel's bare chest, to the place where I'd *bitten* him. I traced it with my finger, and his gaze went silver.

"I wouldn't do that for too long," he growled. "I'll want to take you again, and you have to be sore."

There was a slight twinge between my legs and at my backside, but it just reminded me of what we'd all shared. "I'm not *that* sore."

Cáel chuckled, and the sound wrapped around me like the warmest embrace.

I stilled as I took in a mark below the bite. It looked like an intricate gemstone tattooed on top of the ink that was already there.

"Your brand," Knox explained. "We'll carry it with us always. Just like you'll carry ours."

I glanced down at my chest. The guys had each bitten me at the juncture of my neck and shoulders. The bites themselves were healing already, but I was sure I'd have angry, red teeth marks for a while.

But below them were two unique marks. On the left, where Knox had bitten me, was a swirl inked into my skin. It was beautiful and hypnotic. On the right, where Cáel had claimed me, was a delicate snowflake that looked like a work of art.

I pushed up against the pillows, trying to get a better look. "What do they mean?"

Knox shoved up next to me. "We never know what our mark will be. It can be tied to any number of things." He traced his swirl above my collarbone. "It looks like both of ours tie to our gifts."

I frowned at him. "Gifts?"

Cáel nodded. "Shifters that are especially strong can have extra gifts."

"I can control the air to a certain degree. It gives me extra speed when I'm flying," Knox explained. "And Cáel can control the weather in short bursts."

"The weather?" I squeaked.

Cáel grinned down at me. "I can give you snow whenever you want."

I stared at Knox's arm where I'd bitten him, and my gem was now marked on his bicep. "Will I have a gift?"

"We won't know until you shift. Maybe longer," Knox said.

I dropped my hand from his arm. "And when is that going to be?"

A month ago, I would've been terrified at the prospect, but now I was antsy. I wanted to know what it felt like. And I was starting to feel *something* beneath my skin. A phantom sort of energy pushing to be set free.

Knox stroked his fingers over my belly in a soothing design. "Your dragon has been through a lot. It might take her some time to surface."

"And what if she doesn't?" I asked, finally giving voice to the question that had been swirling about my head for weeks.

"Then she doesn't," Knox said with a shrug.

"But won't you regret mating with me then?"

Cáel let out a rumbling growl. "Never."

Knox slid a hand along my jaw, forcing my gaze to his. "You're ours. It doesn't matter if you never shift. We're honored to be your mate. You've already brought healing to us."

Doubt flickered in my mind, and Knox seemed to read it instantly.

"Even with Easton." Knox's thumb swept back and forth across my cheek. "He's been in denial. Letting his pain and trauma fester. You've forced it to the surface so that he finally has a chance to deal with it."

I wasn't so sure that was a good thing. But maybe.

Cáel linked his fingers with mine. "Knox is right. Your gifts are in far more than you transforming. But I can feel your dragon. She's incredibly strong."

My eyes widened. "You can *feel* her?"

He nodded. "Another one of my gifts is sensing how strong a supernatural is. And I've felt your other half from the moment we met."

I was quiet, trying to sense into myself, to feel something, *anything*. But I came up empty.

I let out an exasperated sigh. "I just want it to happen."

Knox chuckled. "You can't force it. Give her time."

"Easy for you to say," I grumbled. "You've gotten to fly for years."

He bent and brushed his lips against mine. "It'll happen."

"All in good time, Little One," Cáel echoed, kissing my temple.

"But first, we need breakfast. And if we don't hurry, we'll be late for classes," Knox said, sliding out of bed.

Even with the threat of lateness looming, I took a moment to check out his perfectly sculpted ass.

"You're staring, Little One," Cáel said, humor in his voice.

My cheeks heated. "Hey, he's my mate. I'm allowed to stare, right?"

"Damn straight," Knox called as he headed into the bathroom.

I scooted out of bed and stood, freezing. I felt the bite marks at the base of my neck. "Uh, guys?"

Knox poked his head out of the bathroom. "What's wrong?"

"What's wrong is that you left me with something way worse than hickeys. I'm going to have to wear turtlenecks for a month!"

Hayden

IT TURNED OUT THAT, DESPITE FIVE MILLION ARTICLES OF clothing in my closet, there was not one single turtleneck. I'd had to opt for a collared shirt instead. It fully covered the claiming marks, but I couldn't help futzing with it, just to make sure.

Knox finally grabbed my hand and laced his fingers through mine as we headed out of the bedroom. He kissed me quickly. "You look perfect. The bite marks will fade in a matter of days, leaving only a faint scar and the brand behind. No one will know what it is."

I let out a breath. "Okay."

Cáel frowned down at me. "You're nervous."

It was bad enough when the guys could smell things like anxiety and my being turned on, but them actually *feeling* it might bring a whole new slew of problems.

"We took a big step last night. I'm just…adjusting."

Cáel grunted and then moved so fast he was more of a blur than a human form. His large hands dwarfed my face and tugged me to him. He took my mouth, stroking in and demanding a response.

I lost myself in the kiss. There was only Cáel and what he made me feel.

It was only when he pulled back, releasing me, that I realized Knox was still holding my hand. I blinked up at Cáel.

He studied my face. "Not nervous now."

I smacked his chest. "You can't just kiss away my anxiety."

He grinned then. "Just did."

"Whatever," I mumbled. "Someone feed me before I get hangry."

Knox snorted, tugging me down the hallway. "Wouldn't want that."

"Damn straight. I could get violent."

Cáel grinned. "You're vicious, Little One."

"And don't you forget it."

We headed down the stairs and toward the dining room. As we stepped inside, all talking ceased. Three sets of eyes came to us with varied reactions. There was a hint of longing in Maddox's gaze before he quickly masked it. Cillian's jaw was hard as granite as he battled for control. And there was no emotion in Easton at all.

The nerves were suddenly back in full force. Had we done something wrong? Should we not have mated?

Cillian shoved his chair back, dishes clattering with the motion. He rose and stalked toward me. I swallowed hard as those green eyes swirled to black.

Cáel and Knox pushed in on either side, ready to step in if there was any threat of harm.

Cillian let out a low growl at their movements, and Maddox stood, braced for action. Cillian prowled into my space. He lifted a hand to my collar, tugging it to the side. Another sound left his throat as he took in the bite. It was some cross between a growl and a purr.

Cillian traced his lips down my neck until they reached the mark. So gently it made my heart ache, he brushed his mouth across the bite.

A shiver coursed through me, sending sparks of sensation radiating through my muscles. Heat pooled low, and my core tightened.

Cillian pulled me flush against him. He was rock-hard against my belly.

I looked up into those dark eyes, searching. I wasn't sure what I'd find. I worried it might be jealousy or anger, but instead I saw a desperate need.

Cillian's hand fisted in my hair. "Just need a second," he gritted out.

I nodded my head the slightest amount, unsure of how to make this better.

Cillian struggled to breathe normally, and finally, I lifted a hand to his face. He pressed his cheek into my touch, nuzzling. And a bit of the tension in him eased.

I stroked my thumb back and forth across his skin, and Cillian let out another of those noises that sounded like a purr. He dropped his forehead to mine. "Sorry, Little Flame. My dragon is riding me hard this morning."

"Did I hurt you?" I whispered.

Cillian shook his head. "No. It's not that my dragon doesn't want you to bond with my brothers; it's just that he wants it, too. And he's a possessive bastard."

There was a part of me that wanted to offer him the same claiming, here and now. But I knew that wasn't what Cillian wanted. The bonding had to happen when we were both ready, when it felt right.

I pressed up on my tiptoes, kissing him. "I love you."

He lifted me into his arms, soaking in those words. Instead of putting me down, Cillian carried me back to his seat and settled me in his lap.

I frowned up at him. "Um…"

He grinned at me. "Need to feel you close for a bit."

Maddox shook his head as he lowered himself back into his chair. "Possessive bastard is an understatement."

Knox chuckled. "Cill's dragon is probably going to brand her on her forehead."

I twisted in his lap so that I could glare in warning at Cillian. "Don't even think about it. If you give me a face tattoo, I will make it my mission to give you blue balls for the rest of your life."

Cillian laughed, and more of the tension in the room eased. He kissed my temple. "I'll try to rein him in."

"You'd better."

Cáel loaded up a plate full of various breakfast treats. Scrambled eggs, pancakes, sausage. Then he slid it over to me. "OJ or milk?"

"OJ, please."

I reached over for a fork, but Cillian stopped me. I looked up at him in question.

A devilish look entered his eyes. He broke off a piece of pancake with his fingers and dipped it into the syrup. Then he lifted it. "Open."

My mouth opened, part in shock, part in response to that alpha tone.

Cillian slid the bite of food between my lips. "Close," he rasped.

My mouth closed around his fingers, and he took his time pulling them free. Heat swirled around me, need, as the sweet taste flared on my tongue, mixed with that hint of Cillian.

A chair shoved back, making the dishes on the table rattle.

My gaze jerked toward the sound, toward Easton. His eyes cut to me, so much agony swirling there. His chest rose and fell in ragged pants. "I'm sorry. I can't sit by and watch—I can't—"

He cut himself off, storming out of the dining room and slamming the front door. And my happy haze fled with him.

Chapter Thirty-Five

Hayden

Knox and Cáel were sticking close. That, I didn't mind. The fresh bond had me craving their touch and presence all the more. But I hated that I didn't know if they were staying nearby because they wanted that or because they were worried about Easton's stunt.

I could feel Knox's annoyance with his brother, anger even. But I wasn't feeling either of those emotions. I knew that Easton wasn't trying to be an asshole or trying to hurt me. He was in pain. And there was only so much he could take.

The ache in my chest flared, and Cáel let out a growl, pulling me into his side. "I don't know how to make it better."

I burrowed into him. "You can't fix it. But you just being here helps."

Cáel grunted, unhappy with my answer.

"I'm sorry, Hayden," Knox began.

"No," I quickly cut him off. "It's not your fault, and it's not Easton's either."

"The hell it isn't," Knox groused.

"It's not," I pressed. "He's hurting. But I know that you can see he's trying. He's doing everything he can to make the best of a situation he never wanted to be in."

And that *killed*. Because at the end of the day, Easton would never want me. The best-case scenario was that he'd simply give in, and that made me feel gross.

A throat cleared, and I looked up to find Maddox hovering outside his classroom. Worry lined his brow as he studied me. "How are you doing?"

If Mad was finding time in the school day to check in with me, especially in the broad afternoon light, with tons of students around, I knew that I was receiving the full pity party. I tried not to let annoyance at that grab hold. "I'm okay. Really."

I was simply ignoring the fact that Easton had disappeared. I hadn't seen him on campus once today, and I had a feeling he wouldn't be in our upcoming shared class either. I just hoped he was all right.

Maddox's mouth pulled down in a frown. "If you need to cut out early, I can—"

"No. No more missing classes. They honestly help."

Cáel let out another grunt of disagreement.

"Everything's going to be fine," I pushed. But I knew they all heard the lie in my voice.

A bell rang, and I'd never been more grateful.

"I gotta run. Don't want to be late." I started down the hallway, Cáel and Knox on my heels.

When I reached the classroom, Knox tugged me to a stop. He framed my face in his hands. "Wait here after class. We'll meet you as soon as we're out of our seminar."

I nodded in agreement. While I knew the enforcers were patrolling the building, I was past taking chances these days. "See you after class."

Knox kissed me quickly, and Cáel gave me a long hug.

"Slut," someone said, half-covering it with a fake cough.

I pulled out of Cáel's hold to see Delaney walking down the hall with Bella. I rolled my eyes. "Need to work on your originality and delivery," I called.

"I don't hurt women, but I'd like to make an exception for her," Cáel growled.

I patted his chest. "Her punishment is that she actually has to live in her miserable life."

Knox chuckled. "Great point."

I gave them a little wave and headed into the small amphitheater. I scanned the space, disappointment flaring when I didn't see Easton anywhere. Still, I took my normal seat, next to the one he'd been frequenting.

The guy who'd nearly had his ass handed to him by East glared at me. "Where's your bodyguard?"

"I don't see anyone I need a bodyguard for. From what I remember, Easton put you on your ass with his little pinky."

"Burn," one of the guy's friends called with a laugh.

"Bitch," the guy spat, cheeks reddening.

I'd been called worse. Instead of replying, I opened my notebook and readied myself for class.

Professor Brent strode in, gaze sweeping the students. It stopped on me and then the empty seat next to me. He smiled as he set his briefcase down. "Let's begin. We have a lot to cover today."

He wasn't wrong. By the time class was over, my hand ached from all the notes I'd taken. I could've opted for my laptop, but I found I retained things better if I handwrote them.

I took my time as students filed out of class, knowing it would take some time for Cáel and Knox to make it over from the English building anyway. Slipping my notebook into my backpack, I stood and headed down the steps.

"Hayden," Professor Brent called.

I fought the groan that wanted to surface. "Yes, Professor?"

"Let's head to my office. We're overdue for a meeting."

"I actually have plans—"

"They can wait," he clipped.

I bit the inside of my cheek but nodded. Pulling my phone out of my backpack, I typed out a text to Knox and Cáel.

Me: *I have to meet with Professor Brent. Meet me by his office?*

"Let's go," Brent snapped.

I shoved the phone back into my pocket and followed him out of the classroom. It took us a couple of minutes to follow the maze of hallways to his office. He opened the door and gestured me inside.

"Have a seat."

I swallowed hard as he motioned to the couch. I took the spot farthest to one side, placing my backpack in between us to create distance.

Brent scowled at my bag as he sat. "How are you feeling?"

"Good. A lot better." I knotted my fingers together, unsure what the answer should've been for a gunshot victim. I probably should've researched that.

"I'm glad to hear it," Brent said, leaning back against the leather couch. "I've been worried about you."

My stomach twisted. "I'm good, really. All caught up on my schoolwork."

Brent drummed his fingers on the back of the couch. "You know, an advisor's job isn't just to care for their advisee's academic well-being. It's to care for their emotional well-being, as well."

I bit the inside of my cheek. "That's good, too."

He shook his head. "I'm not so sure about that. You've been spending time with some unsavory characters, Hayden. I've heard the rumors."

My breaths came quicker. "I don't think rumors are anything to pay attention to."

Brent arched a brow. "So, you're not involved with multiple men?"

My spine snapped straight. "I'm not sure that's any of your business."

"I'm your advisor."

Anger flared somewhere deep. "And what would the university say if they knew you were asking me about my romantic relationships?"

Anger flashed in the professor's eyes. "I would be perfectly within my rights to be concerned based on what I've heard. In fact, maybe I should bring it up to the university. There is a code of conduct for your scholarship. I'm sure this would go against it."

My blood turned to ice.

A smile stretched across Brent's face, but there was nothing warm about it. "Now, I'm *sure* we can come to some other arrangement."

Bile surged up my throat as Brent shifted to move my backpack.

I jumped to my feet, grabbing the bag and starting for the door.

Brent was faster, though. "Where the hell do you think you're going?"

"Out of here and to report you to the dean," I snapped.

Redness crept up his throat. "You wouldn't dare."

"Move," I ground out, shifting my backpack on my shoulder.

Brent's gaze shifted to my neck, his eyes flaring. "I guess you do like it rough."

And then he lunged.

Chapter Thirty-Six

Hayden

Professor Brent moved so quickly, so unexpectedly, that I didn't have a chance to block his attack. He grabbed me by the throat, shoving me back toward his desk. I batted at his arm, trying to knock it away, but Brent was far stronger than he looked.

I tried to scream, but the sound came out garbled.

Brent tightened his hold on my throat, his other hand slapping across my face in a stinging blow. "You fucking bitch. You think you can tease me, then threaten me?"

The metallic taste of blood filled my mouth as his fingers tightened again.

I kicked out, connecting with Brent's shin.

He cursed, and this time, the blow that connected with my face had me seeing stars.

"You want this," he snarled, tearing at my blouse and sending buttons flying.

I kicked again, this time harder. I landed a shot right be-

The sound that Brent let out wasn't entirely human. He lunged, sending me crashing into the desk. "I'm going to kill you for that."

His hands closed around my throat just as a knock sounded on the door.

"Professor?" Knox called.

I tried to scream, but no sound came out. My vision tunneled as another more insistent knock sounded.

"Professor!"

Spots danced in front of my eyes.

The sound of wood splintering came from far away. Then a roar of fury. And suddenly, the hands at my throat were gone.

I collapsed to the floor, coughing and sputtering. It took a few beats for my vision to come back, but in that time, someone was next to me, hands so incredibly gentle.

"Hayden," Knox croaked. "Oh, God."

I blinked up at him, still coughing.

He hauled me against him, cradling me. "Breathe, baby. Just breathe."

I tried to do that, but they weren't coming easy.

"You think you can touch her?" Cáel roared.

He picked Brent up and threw him against the wall with inhuman strength.

Brent's head cracked against the drywall as he slid down in a heap. True fear filled his eyes as he cowered against Cáel's massive form. "S-she came on to me. I was trying to get her off of me."

"I'm going to be sick," I whispered.

Knox cursed but lifted me in his arms, taking off down the hall. He got me into a single-room bathroom just as the contents of my stomach emptied into the sink. He pulled my hair away from my face as the bile just kept coming.

He trailed a hand up and down my back. "Let it out. That's it. You're okay."

I heaved over and over until my stomach ached and my legs trembled. Knox braced me against the sink as he opened a wooden cabinet next to it. He pulled out a bottle of mouthwash. "This will help."

I nodded weakly as he poured some into a little cup. All I could think was that the staff bathroom was a hell of a lot nicer than the student ones. What a stupid thing to fixate on. But that simple thing was easier to think about than everything…else.

My legs shook harder as I rinsed out my mouth. When I looked in the mirror, I saw my torn blouse, the red marks ringing my neck, and my split lip. Then the tears came.

Knox ripped off his sweatshirt and gently pulled it over my head. "Gonna get you out of here. I'm going to lift you, okay?"

I nodded, unable to speak.

He cradled me in his arms, bracing me to open the door.

Two enforcers charged down the hallway, skidding to a stop in front of us, their eyes going wide.

"Go to Professor Brent's office. Make sure Cáel doesn't kill him here," Knox snapped.

My body trembled harder at the word *kill*.

Knox cursed. "Sorry. I'm so sorry." He walked quickly through the empty hallways, and I prayed we didn't run into any students or staff.

Knox kicked open the back door of the building that led to the parking lot.

The sun shone down. It was in such opposition to the dark events of the day that I couldn't get my brain to compute. None of it made any sense.

My teeth started to chatter.

"Just hold on, Hayden. We're almost there. Gonna get you home. Get you warm," Knox crooned.

"What the hell happened?" a deep voice called. Some part of me recognized it as Easton's. "Terry called and said to meet you at the car."

My vision was blurry as Easton's face filled it. I couldn't exactly make out his features in any defined way, but the rage that permeated bled through all of that.

A snarl twisted his lips. "Who. Did. This?"

Chapter Thirty-Seven

Cael

"Don't kill him. Not here," Terry warned.

The words barely penetrated through the blood roaring in my ears. All I could see was Hayden's face. Her split lip. The bruise already rising on her cheek. The red marks rimming her neck.

"He. Dies," I gritted out.

The pissant scrambled back. "Y-you can't do that. I'm a tenured professor."

I growled low, the sound making everyone in the room freeze. "You. Touched. Her."

"She came on to *me*," Brent snapped.

It was the wrong thing to say.

I lunged forward, my fist connecting with Brent's cheekbone. His head snapped back, hitting the wall. He howled in pain as the door flew open.

Maddox stalked inside. "What the hell is going on?"

"I'm going to sue you!" Brent yelled.

Maddox's gaze jumped from me to the professor and back. "Cáel." He approached me slowly. "What happened?"

I recognized Mad's posture, his tone. It was as if he were approaching an injured animal. He thought I was overreacting to some perceived slight.

"He *attacked* Hayden."

Maddox froze, his eyes swirling gold.

"He's lying!" Brent shouted, scrambling to his feet.

"Where is she?" Maddox demanded.

"Knox has her." Pain flashed through me. The two parts of my soul battled against each other. The need for vengeance, for blood, and the need for *her*.

My jaw worked back and forth as I struggled to get the next words out. "He hit her. Split her lip. Strangled her. Ripped her blouse."

"Lies!" Brent shouted. "She came on to me. I was just trying to get her off me."

Maddox straightened to his full height and turned slowly to face the professor. He stalked forward, each step deliberate, a predator stalking his prey. "She's half your size. You could shove her off with one push. You sure as hell wouldn't have to strangle her. Wouldn't need to rip. Her. Blouse."

"Y-you weren't here. You didn't see," Brent argued.

"I know that Hayden wouldn't touch you with a ten-foot pole. And now I know that you're a sick fuck who's going to pay for his sins in blood," Maddox snarled.

Brent's face reddened. "She's a slut. She was begging for it."

Fury swept through me like an inferno. "What. Did. You. Say?"

My dragon shoved at my skin so hard it was physically painful to hold him back. He wanted to end this human, but he wanted to play with him first.

"Everyone knows that she's fucking everyone who looks her way. Why should I be any different?" Brent huffed.

"I am going to remove your organs one by one, but I'm going

to keep you alive while I do it so that you feel every ounce of agony." My voice had gone completely cold—no warmth in it at all.

Brent paled. But it was too late for him.

My fist struck out again. I went for the temple this time. One carefully placed blow, and he was collapsing to the floor, unconscious.

Maddox glanced at me. "I'm impressed with your control."

"I did it for Hayden," I gritted out. We needed answers before we ended this sack of shit. Needed to make sure he was just your run-of-the-mill monster and not someone the Corbetts had set on Hayden.

Pain streaked across Maddox's face. "How bad was she?"

I tried desperately to shove the images out of my mind. "It wasn't good."

"We called the caster," Pete said, stepping forward. "He's making some salves to help with her healing."

"Cillian wants you to bring the teacher to the shed," Terry added, glaring at the heap on the floor.

My beast pushed for supremacy again. He knew what the shed meant. That he'd get his blood, his screams.

"First, we need to figure out how to get him out of here without being seen," Maddox muttered. "And someone needs to clean up the office so there aren't signs of a struggle."

"I've got an idea," Pete said with a grin. He disappeared out the door, returning a few seconds later with the custodian's cleaning cart. "I think we can make him fit in the garbage can like the trash he is."

Yes, we could.

Our blacked-out SUV pulled up to the rundown shed far from our house. Far enough that no one would hear Brent scream. His muffled yells from the trunk reminded me that my dragon would get to hear every cry of pain. He needed that. Needed to inflict ten times the agony that this monster had inflicted on Hayden.

I opened the back door and slid out of the vehicle, only to be greeted by a very pissed-off Cillian.

"Where. Is. He?" Cillian growled.

"Trunk."

Maddox was already moving to open it as Pete and Terry waited for further instruction.

The back hatch rose as Brent twisted and writhed. But there was tape over his mouth, and his hands and feet were zip-tied.

"Get him in the chair," Cillian snapped.

The two enforcers easily carried a flailing Brent into the shed.

"Have you heard from Knox?" Maddox asked.

Cillian nodded. "He and East are bringing Hayden back to the house now. They'll treat her wounds and make sure she's okay."

"She's not okay." The words ground out like a vicious accusation.

Cillian's eyes bled to black. "I know. And we are going to get retribution."

With that, he stalked toward the shed.

We followed behind to find that Pete and Terry already had the pissant zip-tied to the chair. Cillian prowled toward him, ripping off the tape.

Brent cried out. "I'm going to sue all of you. Take your fucking billions. I'll own your ass."

Cillian chuckled low, sending a shiver over all of us. "They'd have to find your body first. And with the tiny little pieces Cáel is going to chop you into, I highly doubt they will."

Brent's face blanched of all color. "You wouldn't."

"Oh, we would. You're going to die either way. The question is how painful we make it. If you answer me honestly now, I'll make sure it's quick. If you fuck with me, I'll let Cáel take his time."

My dragon surged again. He wanted to keep the monster alive for days, to stretch out the torture for as long as possible.

"Y-you're messing with me," Brent stammered.

"Am I?" Cillian asked, extending his hand toward Terry, who placed a knife in it. In one swift movement, Cillian brought the knife down. It cleanly severed one of Brent's fingers.

There was a pause and then a scream of agony.

Cillian grinned, wiping the blade on Brent's pants. "Now. Are you going to tell me what I want to know?"

"Yes! Yes! Fuck!"

"Good. Who told you to target Hayden?"

Brent's brow puckered. "What? No one."

Cillian pressed the blade to his throat. "You sure about that?"

"Y-yes. She's hot. I just thought—she seemed like she liked me."

Maddox and I let out audible growls that had Brent's eyes widening.

"Do you know the Corbett family?" Cillian asked, fury lacing his tone.

"Who? No. Do they have a kid at the school?"

Brent didn't know shit. He was just a sick fuck trying to prey on his advisees.

Cillian stepped back, looking at me. "Cáel, he's all yours."

"But you said!" Brent yelled.

Cillian glared at him. "I lied."

I brought my hand down, unsheathing my claws.

Brent's eyes went wide as saucers. "W-what are you?"

I grinned. "Your worst nightmare."

Chapter Thirty-Eight

Hayden

I trembled against Knox as the SUV bumped over the gravel road. The divots in the ground just made me shake harder. All I could think about was how cold I felt. The kind of cold where your bones felt brittle.

Knox pulled me closer against him. "You're safe, Hayden. We've got you."

The faintest whimper left my lips. I hated the sound, the sign of weakness, but I couldn't pull it back.

"How's she doing?" Easton asked from the driver's seat. Tension radiated through his voice like a live wire.

"She's in shock. Shaking like a goddamned leaf," Knox growled.

Easton's fingers tightened on the steering wheel, bleaching white. "I hope Cill lets Cáel loose on him."

I pressed tighter into Knox's chest. I didn't want to be the reason for Cáel losing another piece of himself. But I also didn't want to see Professor Brent ever again.

Memories slammed into me. His hands on my throat. My shirt tearing.

Knox's lips ghosted over my hair. "We're almost home. Almost there." His head lifted. "Faster."

"I don't want to hurt her with the potholes," Easton muttered.

"We just need to get her home. Pete texted that Marcus left healing balms for us there."

Healing balms. I had no doubt that the caster would've made something that would erase all evidence of what had happened to me. I wondered if he could make something that erased the memories, too. I didn't want to see Brent's face twisted with rage or see the intent in those dark eyes.

I shuddered against Knox.

"What can I do?" he begged. "What do you need?"

"C-cold," I whispered.

Knox tried to cover more of my body with his. "We'll get you into a bath as soon as we get home. That'll warm you right up. Then we'll get the balm on you and into bed."

I nodded jerkily as we passed through the open gates to the guys' territory. Open but with several guards standing sentry.

It only took Easton a matter of minutes to get us to the house. He took each turn like a racecar driver before skidding to a stop by the front door and sending gravel flying.

Easton was out of the driver's seat in a flash, coming around to open the back door. Knox slid out with me in his arms. He carried me as if I weighed no more than a feather. But with shifter strength, maybe that was all I felt like.

Easton jogged ahead to open the front door, and Knox carried me inside.

Knox inclined his head toward a set of jars on the hutch in the foyer. "Those must be the balms."

Easton nodded, grabbing them and following us up the stairs.

Knox carried me toward my bedroom. The familiar sights and smells should've eased my anxiety, but it still had me in a vicious grip. And the cold wouldn't let go.

Knox made his way through my bedroom and into the

bathroom, flicking on the light. He carefully set my feet on the floor. "Can you stand? I'm going to run you a bath."

I bobbed my head in a nod. But as he stepped away, I started to falter.

Strong arms came around me. "I've got you," Easton whispered.

My whole body trembled. "C-cold. So cold." My teeth chattered violently, and Easton cursed.

"We have to get her warm," he told Knox.

"I know. Running the bath now," Knox shot back.

"Okay, Hayden. We need to get you out of those clothes. Can we do that?" Easton asked gently.

I nodded again, but the movement was some sort of staccato motion that barely made sense.

"All right. Can you lift your arms for me?"

I did as he asked, and Easton carefully lifted the sweatshirt over my head. As his eyes narrowed on my torn shirt, they bled to gold, and his breathing became ragged as he battled back his rage. He swallowed hard. "Shirt, okay?"

"'Kay," I whispered.

Easton slid the shirt off my shoulders, and the ruined garment fell to the floor.

Knox moved in beside us, dropping to his knees. "I'm going to get your jeans, okay?"

I nodded in that deranged way again.

His fingers moved quickly, removing my shoes and then my pants and underwear.

My fingers fisted in Easton's T-shirt as I shook even harder. "Don't let go," I begged.

He pulled me into him. "I've got you. Not letting go."

Knox stood then, unfastening my bra and managing to get it free, even with Easton holding me. "Tub's full enough."

I felt Easton nod more than saw it.

"Hayden, can I get you into the tub?" he asked.

The shaking was back in full force, but maybe it had never gone away. I didn't want to be alone. Didn't want the memories to come. "Don't let go."

It was all I could say.

Easton cursed, lifting me into his arms as he kicked off his shoes.

"What are you doing?" Knox asked.

"Keeping my promise." Easton strode toward the massive tub and stepped into it with me in his arms. He somehow managed to lower us both into the water.

It was so hot it scalded my freezing skin. I let out a whimper.

He stilled. "Too hot?"

I shook my head violently. I needed that warmth.

"Okay. We're getting in together." Easton lowered us deeper into the water. His jeans were soaked now. Then half of his tee. But he didn't seem to give a damn.

Finally, we were fully submerged. Easton cradled me against his chest as the warmth seeped into me, and the shaking eased a fraction. "That's my girl. Nice and warm. I've got you. I'm not letting go."

Chapter Thirty-Nine

Easton

EVEN THOUGH THE WORST OF THE SHAKING HAD EASED, A slight tremble still radiated through Hayden's body. A tremble that had me wanting to slice that piece of shit to ribbons.

I struggled to keep my breathing even, not to let my fury win. Cillian, Maddox, and Cáel would deal with Brent. Hayden needed me right now.

I stilled at that thought. She needed me.

A war of fear and hope raged in my chest. But it was a war I was losing. It was too hard to stay away from Hayden. Especially now.

Guilt hit fast and hard. If I'd been in class like I should've been, Brent wouldn't have gotten her alone. None of this would've happened.

"East," Knox said softly.

My twin read me clear as day.

"I should've been there," I whispered hoarsely.

"We all should've been."

My throat worked as I swallowed. I'd never forgive myself for this.

Hayden let out another whimper as her body relaxed more against mine.

"She's asleep," Knox said quietly.

"Good. It's what she needs."

Knox studied us for a moment. "Let's keep her in there for a few more minutes. She needs to get fully warm."

"The shaking's better."

He nodded. "The adrenaline's leaving her system."

Adrenaline because she was fighting for her life, fighting not to be violated in the worst possible way.

The fury was back, and scales rippled over my arms. "Have you heard from Cillian?"

Knox pulled his phone out of his back pocket, scanning the screen. "They've got him in the shed."

"Good," I clipped.

I knew what the shed meant. He wouldn't come out of that place breathing. God, I hoped Cáel took his time with the sicko. I hoped he made his ending as painful as possible.

Knox glanced at me. "I'm gonna get you both some dry clothes. You going to be okay for a minute?"

I nodded, and he headed out of the bathroom.

My fingers trailed up and down Hayden's spine. Her skin was so unbelievably smooth. Delicate. Just like her. But that delicateness hid a strength.

Knox had told me that it had been clear Hayden had fought back. Fought against someone twice her size and had gotten in a few good licks. God, I wanted her to shift so that she had that increased strength. So that human assholes wouldn't stand a chance against her. It wouldn't help that much against other shifters, but at least it would be more of an even match.

Footsteps sounded, and Knox reappeared with a pair of sweats and a tee for me and some pajamas for Hayden. He set them on the counter. "Ready to get her out?"

No. I wasn't. Because with Hayden in my arms, I knew she was safe. Whole.

"Sure," I lied.

I brushed the hair away from her face. "Hayden?"

"Mmm," she mumbled.

"I'm going to lift you out of the bath, okay?"

"'Kay," she said, smacking her lips but not quite fully awake.

I stood, the air feeling cold after the warmth of the bath. Knox was immediately there with a towel, taking Hayden from my arms. But I didn't want to give her up. The only thing letting me do so was knowing that she needed to get dry and warm.

I quickly shucked my soaking wet clothes and dropped them into the draining bathtub so they wouldn't get water everywhere. I grabbed a towel, drying myself as fast as possible before putting on the sweats.

"Grab the pajamas," Knox called.

I did and headed back to him and Hayden. Her eyes were glassy as she blinked up at me. "Thank you."

A muscle along my jaw fluttered. "You don't have to thank me."

She shouldn't. Not when I should've been there to stop it from happening in the first place.

I handed the pajama bottoms to Knox as I opened the top. "Let's get this on you."

I studiously avoided Hayden's chest, focusing on getting her arms into the sleeves and then wrapping it around her. Slowly, my fingers fastened each button. But as I reached the top button, my gaze locked on the angry red marks on her throat. They were already deepening to bruises.

"Grab me the balm," I croaked to Knox as he rose from getting Hayden's pajama bottoms on.

He jerked his head in a nod and crossed to where I'd set the two jars. He handed me one. "This is for any bruising. I've got the one for her lip."

I unscrewed the lid and dabbed a glob of it onto my finger. My gaze locked with Hayden's. "Tell me if anything hurts."

"Okay," she whispered.

As gently as possible, I rubbed it over the marks. God, I hoped this erased any pain, any reminder of what had happened to her. The scent of it had a hint of rose. A hell of a lot better than the stuff we'd gotten our hands on before.

I finished smoothing it over Hayden's neck and then put a dab on her cheek where another bruise was forming. "I'm so sorry, Hayden."

"Not your fault," she said hoarsely.

But it was. And I'd never forget that.

"Come on," Knox said, wrapping an arm around her waist. "Let's get you into bed."

She let Knox guide her into the bedroom as I wiped my fingers clean on a towel. By the time I followed, Hayden was settled into the middle of the giant bed, and Knox was settling in next to her.

Hayden's eyelids fluttered as she curled into Knox, already slipping back into sleep. It was what she needed most right now.

Knox's gaze locked with mine. "Stay."

My throat worked as I swallowed. Leaving was the first thing I should've done.

But I didn't.

I walked to the bed and slid in on Hayden's other side, Knox watching me the entire time.

"Are you okay?"

I shook my head. "But it doesn't matter anymore." I was going to have to learn to live with my raging demons. Because my heart chose her, even though my brain told me she'd bring me to ruin. I'd just have to go down in the flames.

CHAPTER FORTY

Hayden

HEAT COCOONED ME ON ALL SIDES, AND I LET OUT A nonsensical mumble as I blinked against the morning light. And I kept right on blinking at the sight that greeted me. I had to be dreaming. That was the only answer that made any sense.

Because the sight in front of me was something I'd been sure I'd never see. Easton was propped against the pillows, facing me. His long hair was mussed from sleep, curling around his shoulders in that gorgeous mix of browns and blonds. My fingers itched to touch it, but I knew that would break the dream.

"How do you feel?" he asked gruffly.

I blinked again. "I'm dreaming."

Easton frowned. "No…"

A chuckle sounded behind me. "Not dreaming, baby." Knox pressed a kiss to my shoulder as he sat up in bed.

I struggled to do the same. My body protested the action a bit. My muscles ached as if I'd gone on an especially rough roller-coaster ride, which had memories surging to the surface.

I squeezed my eyes closed, trying to fight them back.

Knox took my hand in an instant. "You're okay. You're safe."

"Safe," I whispered, trying to get myself to believe it.

Slowly, I opened my eyes to meet concerned green ones. Easton had shifted so that he was facing me. "Do you need medicine? Is anything hurting?"

I lifted my hand to my lip. The place where it had split didn't show any sign of injury. Then my fingers dropped to my neck. I carefully prodded the skin there, but there was no pain.

"Marcus made you a few things to help with healing," Knox explained.

The vague memory of him and Easton treating my wounds filled my mind. A soaking wet Easton.

My gaze flicked up to his. "You got into the bath with me."

He'd ignored the fact that he was fully clothed and simply got right in. The memory had my heart twinging at his kindness.

"You needed someone."

And for Easton, it was as simple as that.

"Thank you."

That had him scowling. "You don't need to thank me."

"All right…" I turned to Knox. "What happened to, um, you know?"

I couldn't find it in myself to say my advisor's name, too scared it would send me spiraling again.

Knox and Easton were quiet for a moment. It was Easton who finally cleared his throat. "He's been dealt with."

"Dealt with…" My words trailed off as things became clear. "Oh."

Knox pressed a kiss to my temple. "Don't have a moment's guilt. Behavior like this. It's never a one-off. We're ridding the world of someone who would go on to hurt countless more women."

My stomach twisted at the thought. Knox was right. There was no way I was the first, and I certainly wouldn't have been the last. I doubted Brent's previous victims had the kind of support and backup I did. They'd likely had to deal with it alone.

But I wasn't alone. Not anymore.

"Knox is right," Easton gritted out. "Death is a kindness for that piece of shit."

My focus shifted to him, really taking him in. I could see the fury beneath the surface, but I could also see the concern. For me.

"Not going to argue with you there."

He just grunted. "Are you hurting?"

I shook my head. "Not really."

"So, yes," Easton said, starting to rise.

I grabbed his arm, stopping him. "Just a little muscle soreness. Nothing that requires medication."

Easton studied me for a moment, trying to read whether I was telling him the truth.

"I'm not a martyr. I'd tell you if I needed the good stuff."

I was hoping for a flicker of humor in his expression, but there wasn't even a hint.

"I'm okay," I promised. And physically, I was. But I knew that mentally and emotionally, it was going to take some time.

Easton lifted a hand to brush the hair out of my face. "You need time to rest and heal."

"Don't we need to keep up our normal schedules? I'm not an expert on getting away with murder, but that seems like a good place to start."

Knox chuckled. "She has a point."

"I don't have morning classes today, so I've got a few hours before I need to be on campus," I said when Easton scowled again.

"We don't have anything until eleven," Knox said. "We can have a good breakfast and take it easy until we leave for campus."

"Fine," Easton huffed.

My lips twitched. "Thank you for worrying."

The scowl just deepened. "Stop thanking me."

"You can't control who I thank. I'm just letting you know that I appreciate your concern."

He huffed out a breath. "Okay."

Easton was quiet for a moment before slowly lifting a hand to my face. "I'm so glad you're okay."

My breath hitched as my heart sped up.

Easton's throat worked as he swallowed. "I can't stay away from you anymore, Hayden. I tried. So damned hard. But you smashed through every defense."

A war erupted inside me. One part of me howled in victory. But the other part had me frowning…

Wariness flitted across Easton's expression. "What's wrong?"

I worried the inside of my cheek as I searched for the right words. "I want you to want me for *me,* not because the bond broke you."

"The bond didn't break me. You did. Because of who you are."

I shook my head, scooting out of his touch. The loss of his hand on my face killed me. "You don't even *know* me. Because you've been hell-bent on keeping me at arm's length."

Easton's eyes flashed. "I know you, Hayden. Like I know my own soul. That's what a true mate is."

"But I want to be more to you than a true mate. I want to be the person you *choose*. Not just someone who's been forced on you."

Chapter Forty-One

Knox

Easton's expression closed down at Hayden's words. "You weren't forced on me."

She arched a brow in challenge. "Really? Because that's what you've treated me like from day one."

He snapped his mouth closed. Because there wasn't any argument to be made. Hayden was completely right. Easton might be coming around now, but his actions had consequences.

He shoved off the bed and stalked toward the door, slamming it behind him.

Hayden's shoulders slumped as she curled in on herself.

I had the burning urge to deck Easton all over again. Wrapping my arms around her, I pulled Hayden into me. "It's going to be okay."

"Am I a massive bitch?"

"Hey, don't talk about my mate that way." My fingers stroked over my claiming mark and down to the swirl of air below it. I'd never get tired of seeing my brand on her skin.

"He was sort of trying, in his own way," Hayden mumbled against my chest.

"He hurt you," I said softly. Just saying the words killed. To know that my brother, my twin, had done such damage to the woman I loved.

Hayden's fingers traced the gemstone on my bicep, sending a shiver of pure pleasure through me. "He did. I know it's complicated, though. Hurting me wasn't personal. But I can't just magically forget that it ever happened. And he hasn't taken the time to get to know me."

I held her tighter. "I get that." My lips brushed over her temple again. "Just give him a chance to get to know you, okay?"

I didn't have any right to ask this of Hayden, but I did it anyway. Because I couldn't stand seeing her or my brother in pain. And they both would be until they figured this thing out.

Hayden tipped her head back so that she could see my eyes. "You're a softie, you know that?"

I gave her a mock scowl. "No. I'm ferocious and terrifying."

She giggled. "I'm shaking in my boots."

Leaning in, I nipped her bottom lip lightly. "You should be."

Hayden answered the nip by pressing her mouth to mine. My tongue stroked in on instinct, but I forced myself not to take things any further. She'd been through too much yesterday. When I finally pulled away, Hayden's eyes were slightly glassy.

"You're good at kissing."

I chuckled. "Glad you think so." The humor left my tone. "How are you feeling? *Really?*"

Hayden reached up and stroked my jaw. "I'm okay. I know I'll have to deal more with the emotional side of things, but having you and the rest of our bond…it makes me feel safe."

I pressed my forehead to hers, breathing in her jasmine scent. "I'm glad. But you know that if you ever need to talk about anything, I'm always here."

"I know," Hayden whispered. "I love you, Knox. Thank you for helping me feel like I belong. For giving me a home."

My heart jerked in my chest. My brave, beautiful girl. She'd been through so much. I wished I could erase it all. "Wish you could feel how much I love you."

"I do. I feel it every single day in everything you do."

Everything in me twisted. "I need to let you go or we're never going to leave this bed."

Hayden's stomach growled at that.

I laughed. "Okay, you get ready. I'll meet you in the dining room. I need to go find East."

Her brows pulled together. "He doesn't hate me, right?"

"No. He doesn't hate you."

The problem was that Easton was falling in love with Hayden, and it was freaking him the hell out.

She nodded and slid out of bed. "I'll meet you for breakfast."

Hayden disappeared into the bathroom, and I hurried to pull on my jeans. I followed Easton's scent down the hall to his bedroom. I didn't bother knocking. I knew he'd just tell me to go away.

Opening the door, I found him staring out the window at the forest.

"I know Mom taught you to knock."

"You'd just tell me to fuck off."

"You said it, not me," Easton muttered.

I crossed to him and gave him a little shove. "Stop being a sulky baby."

Easton glared at me, the gold in his eyes sparking. "I told her I wanted to be with her, and she rejected me."

I scoffed. "You basically told her that you wanted nothing to do with her, but the bond broke down your defenses, and you expected her to fall at your feet."

"I didn't—"

"You did." I sighed. "You know I love you, East. But you've

been a real asshole to Hayden. You've hurt her. It's going to take time to prove that you're truly in this. And for *her* and not just the bond."

Pain streaked across Easton's face. "I didn't mean to hurt her. I just—I couldn't—"

"You were scared."

His gaze connected with mine. "I was fucking terrified. I still am."

I gripped my twin's shoulder. "Don't let the fear win."

"I'm trying. But it's hard. When I saw her yesterday, everything in me shredded. It was the worst kind of pain."

"Because you care about her."

"And there's a part of me that wishes I didn't."

My back teeth ground together. "She feels that, East. We're too connected for her not to."

Easton cursed and began to pace. "I can't just turn it off."

"I know that. But you do have control of your actions. Get to know her. Spend time with her. Make her feel like you're invested in the relationship. Even if it's hard for you."

Easton's pacing slowed, and he finally came to a stop. "Why do I feel like you're telling me to grow some balls?"

I grinned. "Because I am."

This time, Easton gave me a shove. "You're such an ass."

"No, I'm a good brother who's going to give you the hard truth. If you want Hayden, you're going to have to win her."

Chapter Forty-Two

Hayden

I skimmed my hands over the blouse I'd paired with jeans, checking my reflection for the tenth time. The bruises and split lip were completely gone. But I'd still have to be careful to hide my claiming marks until they faded into faint scars. The brands just looked like tattoos, so those would have an easy enough explanation at least.

Staring at myself in the mirror, I huffed out a breath. "Stop being such a chicken."

I swallowed hard and turned away from my reflection. Making my way through my bedroom, I headed for the hallway. When I reached the top of the stairs, I could hear the faint strains of voices. My stomach flipped.

I hadn't seen Cillian, Cáel, and Maddox since my attack. I knew they'd been dealing with…*him*. I was grateful for that, but I didn't want them to look at me differently.

Squaring my shoulders, I descended the stairs and moved toward the dining room. The moment I stepped inside, all talking halted.

I hovered in the entryway for a moment. "Uh, hi."

Cáel was on his feet in a flash, striding toward me. His gaze roamed, checking for any sign of injury. When he didn't see any, he hauled me into his arms. "Little One," he rasped.

I hugged him hard. "I'm okay. I promise."

He buried his face in my neck, breathing me in. His body shuddered on the exhale.

I just held him for a minute, hoping that the contact would help. Finally, I pulled back a fraction, needing to see his face.

I lifted a hand, tracing it over his features. My fingers ghosted under his eyes, where there were dark smudges. "You didn't sleep."

Cáel gave a small shake of his head. "I needed to let my dragon out. Yesterday was...a lot for him. When he gets into those states, I need to fly until he's exhausted."

I frowned at him. "But now you're exhausted, too."

Cáel leaned down and pressed a kiss to my forehead. "I'll be okay as long as I know you are."

"I am."

A throat cleared, and I found Cillian standing next to us. He, too, had dark circles under his eyes. I moved from Cáel's hold and wrapped my arms around him.

Cillian engulfed me in his massive frame. "Are you really okay?"

I nodded against him. "But you aren't."

"Long few days," he muttered.

More like weeks. I turned my head to press a kiss over his heart. "I've missed you."

"You have no idea, Little Flame."

Warmth spread through me at his words, and I burrowed deeper into his hold. "I'm right here whenever you need me."

"Thank you," he rasped.

We stood there for another few moments, just holding each other, Cáel's heat at my back. When Cillian finally released me, I realized Maddox had joined our little group.

He shuffled his feet, looking down. The move was so un-Maddox-like. Maddox was usually calm confidence. He was never unsure.

Finally, he looked up, meeting my gaze. "I'm so sorry."

I frowned at him. "You didn't do anything—"

Maddox cut me off with a sharp shake of his head. "I knew that Brent's female advisees didn't usually stick around. I thought it was because he was a misogynist, but I should've looked closer. Should've known there was more going on."

"So, you're blaming yourself because you're not psychic?" I challenged.

Maddox's brows rose. "No, I—"

"Good. Because that would be really freaking dumb, and I thought you were the genius around here."

His lips twitched. "Can't let that reputation falter."

"No, you can't."

Maddox reached out, his hand curling around mine. The simple touch sent a wave of heat through me. Prickles of sensation danced through my palm. "I'm glad you're okay. Glad you fought."

My throat worked as I swallowed. "Me, too."

Footsteps sounded in the hallway, and Maddox dropped my hand. It was as if a gaping hole appeared in my chest the moment I lost the contact. Those tiny pieces of Maddox meant more to me than was logical. But I'd hold on to them with everything I had.

"What's going on?" Knox asked. "Why are you all standing around when there's food on the table?"

Cillian chuckled. "One-track mind."

I glanced past Knox at Easton. I braced for animosity after the way he'd stormed out of my bedroom earlier. But there wasn't any to be found. He moved forward and dropped a kiss to the top of my head. "Want me to fix you a plate?"

Everyone around us stilled.

"Uh, no. That's okay. I can do it." My words tripped over each other.

Easton nodded. "Just make sure you get enough to eat. You missed dinner last night."

I'd slept right through it, and my stomach was ravenous. I made my way to the table, taking my usual seat. Easton followed behind me, stealing Knox's spot before he could grab it.

Knox ducked his head to hide his grin, opting for the opposite side of the table. Cheeky bastard.

I scooped eggs onto my plate, along with a croissant that looked amazing, and a fruit salad that seemed to have all the colors of the rainbow. As I started to eat, I glanced at Cillian. "Is, uh, everything taken care of with you-know-who?"

Cillian's fingers tightened around his fork. "Yes. He won't be an issue anymore. If anyone asks if you've seen him, just say you had a meeting after class and that Knox picked you up from it. You guys didn't see Brent after that."

It wasn't even a lie. Knox had literally picked me up from the meeting. A shiver washed through me as the memories tried to surface.

Knox cleared his throat. "We have the morning off. What do you want to do? We could go shopping or go for a hike."

"She should rest," Easton argued.

I sent a sidelong glance in his direction. "I feel completely fine. And I think I slept for like fifteen hours."

Easton frowned but nodded.

I broke off a piece of my croissant. "There is one thing I'd like to do."

Cillian turned to me. "Name it."

And I knew he meant that. He would move heaven and earth to give me my heart's desires.

I smiled at him. "Can I meet your dragons?"

Chapter Forty-Three

Hayden

BIRDS SANG OVERHEAD AS WE ALL MADE OUR WAY INTO the massive clearing. Everyone but Maddox. He'd made an excuse about needing to get to campus to grade papers, but I couldn't help but feel like he was pushing me away. Or at least setting a boundary. He wasn't ready for me to meet his dragon.

I tried not to let that sting. I knew things were complicated for him. But I wondered if his faculty position was just a convenient excuse.

I turned around, taking in the woods around us. "It's beautiful out here."

Cillian grinned. "One of our favorite spots. There's a swimming hole not too far that way once it gets warmer."

That sounded amazing. I couldn't wait to explore their territory. I bet there were countless treasures hidden away.

Knox moved in next to me. "You sure about this?"

I nodded, a smile pulling at my lips. "I want to meet them."

"We won't be able to communicate with you, just with each

"How?" I asked.

One corner of Knox's mouth kicked up. "We can mind-speak when we're in dragon form."

My jaw went slack. "Seriously? Will I be able to do that?"

"That and more," Cillian assured me.

"This is so freaking cool."

Cáel chuckled, dropping a kiss to my head. "I can't wait to meet *your* dragon."

"You and me both," I muttered. I was getting more and more antsy for her to surface. I wanted to know what it felt like to shift. To *fly*.

"Okay," Cillian called. "Everyone ready?"

The guys nodded. Easton had been mostly quiet through breakfast, but he'd been present. Every now and then, he'd ask a question that told me he was paying attention.

He was the first to tug his tee over his head. I gaped at the defined planes of muscle. Silver barbells glinted in his nipples. Their presence had heat pooling low in my belly. Along his side was a large yet intricate tattoo. It read *Teaghlach* in a script that looked like art.

Easton shot me a grin that had my cheeks heating, and I quickly averted my eyes. But everywhere I looked, there were muscled bodies on display. I finally ducked my head to stare at the ground.

"Holy hell," I muttered to myself. These guys were going to kill me.

A second later, I heard a cracking and popping sound. Then another. And another.

My gaze lifted just in time to see Cillian transform into a massive pitch-black dragon with white eyes. He was both terrifying and enchanting.

He let out a huff of air but didn't move. I realized then that he was waiting for me. I didn't hesitate.

Crossing the clearing, I approached him slowly. I held out a hand just shy of his snout. Cillian closed the distance, bumping it with his head the way a dog would when it wanted pets.

A laugh bubbled out of me as I stroked his head. I wasn't sure what I was expecting, but Cillian's scales were as smooth as silk. But warm, too. Warmer than a human's skin. Was that because they had the ability to breathe fire?

"You're so soft," I whispered.

Cillian let out a sound that resembled a sort of purr. But because he was so large, it made the ground around us tremble.

A huff sounded behind me, and I turned to see a white dragon with a silver sheen. I knew this one was Cáel. Even if I hadn't seen him transform before, the pale blue eyes would've told as much.

I smiled as I moved toward him. Of course, Cáel was impatient for pets.

I approached him from the side, making my way toward his long neck. I stroked a hand down it. Cáel was just as soft as Cillian. I leaned into him, pressing my face to his scales. The warmth seeped into me.

Cáel let out a growl that could only be classified as…happy. My Angry Marshmallow.

I hugged his neck, even though my arms didn't make it halfway around his circumference. When I let go, I leaned into him, taking in the rest of the clearing.

Two other dragons peered back at me. Both were green and gold with golden eyes. Their markings matched their eyes in human form, so I could instantly tell them apart.

Pushing off Cáel, I headed for the one with more green on his scales. "Knox," I greeted, holding out a hand.

I swore the damned dragon grinned. Then he butted my hand. I stroked his face, then scratched under his chin.

Knox's back leg thumped furiously.

I laughed. "Like that spot, huh?"

The second dragon moved in closer.

I let my hand drop from Knox and turned toward Easton. His

dragon's eyes were curious, the emotion in them lighter than his human counterpart. He nosed the air.

My mouth curved as something shifted in my chest. I didn't feel any of the same reservations with this animal that I did with human Easton. There was no urge to protect myself or wonder about his motives.

I closed the distance between us and lifted a hand to scratch behind his ear. Easton let out a sound that was part rumbling growl, part purr. I only grinned wider.

As I scratched that spot, Easton's wings fluttered. I watched in fascination as the almost-translucent appendages moved through the air. They were incredible.

My hand stilled on Easton, and I turned around.

"Can you take me flying?"

Chapter Forty-Four

Hayden

The four dragons in the clearing froze. A second later, both Easton and Cáel started shaking their massive heads. While they couldn't speak, they were making their displeasure at the idea of me flying known.

"Come on," I begged. "I've been dying to. And maybe it'll help me connect with my dragon."

Knox looked to Cillian, who seemed to be mulling over the idea.

Easton clearly didn't care for his brother's reaction because he headbutted him and nipped his ear.

Knox roared at Easton, shoving him off.

The sound was so loud, I stumbled back a few steps.

Easton didn't like this either, and he charged at his brother. They rolled in a tangle of limbs and wings until Cillian let out a deafening roar.

My hands flew to my ears as the twins froze. Slowly, they extricated themselves from the heap and ducked their heads. They looked so sheepish. Like two little puppies caught chewing on a pair of slippers.

I couldn't help it. I giggled. They both looked at me curiously.

"You're like puppies being scolded," I explained.

Easton let out a huff, not caring for the comparison.

I just grinned wider. "I'm sorry. You'll always be Mr. Grumpy Cat to me."

That had his eyes narrowing, but I didn't miss the amusement there.

Knox watched me and his brother carefully, and I didn't miss the hope in his expression.

But I didn't want the weight of that on my shoulders. I turned to Cillian. "Will you take me flying?"

I knew it was he who would have the final say. He was the alpha, after all.

I started toward him, determined to make my case. But Cáel cut me off, letting out a chuffing sound.

Pinning him with a stare, I placed my hands on my hips. "Don't think you can bully me with your size, even if you are one million times bigger."

Cáel still didn't move.

I tried to dart around him, but he was surprisingly agile for being so large, and he cut me off again. I was going to need a different game plan.

Searching around me, I bent and picked up a fallen branch from one of the pine trees. It wasn't very large, but I thought the needles just might do the trick. I brushed them down the side of Cáel's neck.

He jerked and twisted, letting out a barking laugh. The moment I had an opening, I booked it to Cillian. *Thank goodness for ticklish dragons.*

Cáel let out a growl of frustration, but Cillian was grinning, showing all his razor-sharp teeth.

"Did I earn my flight?" I asked hopefully.

Cillian tossed his head back, motioning to his back. I didn't hesitate. It took a few tries to make it up Cillian's back, but finally, I succeeded, settling just above his wings. I searched for something to hold on to, anything.

Finally, I saw what was almost a braid of scales along his neck. I touched it gently. "Will it hurt if I grab these?"

Cillian shook his head.

I wrapped it around my hand until I was sure I was secure. Then I patted Cill's neck. "I'm ready."

Cáel and Easton let out sounds of protest, but I ignored them.

Cillian stood, his large body moving to the center of the clearing. His wings began to flap, sending a gust of air over me. Then we were rising.

"Oh my God," I whispered.

In a matter of seconds, we were hovering over the trees, and then we were flying.

Cillian dipped and swooped as he picked up speed. The wind stung my face as he shot forward. I felt completely weightless and… *right.*

Something stirred inside me. An awakening of sorts at just how at home I felt in the sky.

A few seconds later, three other dragons joined us. Cáel on one side, Easton and Knox on the other. Cillian led the formation, taking us over the forest toward the mountains.

I grinned as he dipped down to a waterfall, the spray splashing my face. Then he was up again and soaring. That weightless feeling was back and along with it, complete bliss.

Was this what my parents had been hiding from me? I couldn't imagine staying away from this form if I had it. But maybe they'd done it for me.

Cillian dove, and I let out a happy shriek as my stomach dipped with him. Then he was back to hovering just above the treetops.

Knox rose above us, his form casting a massive shadow. I

reached up with my free hand, trailing my fingers over his belly. Knox let out a roar of pleasure. As he peeled off, he rewarded me with a flip that had me grinning from ear to ear.

We flew for at least an hour, until I finally patted Cillian's neck in a sign to go home. My arms were aching, and I didn't want to take a tumble.

The rest of the guys stayed at our side as we headed home. As Cillian lowered us to the clearing once again, I caught sight of a figure standing off to the side.

I beamed as I slid off Cillian's back. "Mad, it was amazing! I flew! We went to a waterfall and around the mountains and—"

My words cut off as I took in Maddox's face. There was no hint of levity in his eyes. "What's wrong?"

He swallowed hard, looking to the men behind me still in their dragon forms. "The police were on campus. They want to talk to Hayden."

Chapter Forty-Five

Hayden

I TWISTED MY FINGERS TOGETHER IN INTRICATE KNOTS AS trees flew past the SUV's windows.

"Let's go over the game plan," Cillian said from behind the wheel. His voice would've sounded calm to just about everyone else. But I could hear the tension wrapping around his vocal cords.

"We should get our lawyer on this," Easton groused from the seat behind me.

Maddox shook his head. "If we throw our overpriced shark on this, the cops are instantly going to look harder at Hayden."

My knuckles blanched white, all the blood leaving them.

Cáel covered my hand with his. "It's going to be okay."

I nodded, but there was nothing in me that believed him.

Cillian's gaze flicked to the rearview mirror. As he took me in, a muscle in his cheek popped. "Mad is right. For now, we play innocent. If they want to talk to Hayden again, then we get the lawyer involved."

There were several sounds of assent throughout the vehicle.

"Good," Cillian clipped. "Knox will play the doting boyfriend."

Knox shot me a smug grin. "That's going to be a *real* hardship."

Cáel sent a growl in his direction.

I squeezed his hands with my fingers. "*Play*. That doesn't change what you are to me, too."

He let out a little huff.

"I'll be taking the role of overprotective big brother," Cillian went on. "And Mad, the liaison to the university."

"What about me and Cáel?" Easton asked.

"You guys are going to keep your distance. It would look weird as hell if all five of us showed up." Cillian's gaze flicked to Cáel through the rearview mirror. "And your dragon is too close to the surface after the ordeal with Brent."

The snarl that left Cáel's lips was more menacing than I'd heard before. I twisted in my seat, pressing a hand to his cheek. "Look at me," I pleaded.

Cáel didn't move for a moment.

I swiped my thumb back and forth across his cheek. "Cáel," I whispered. "Come back to me."

Slowly, his focus moved from Cillian down to me. His eyes were almost completely silver.

"We're being strategic. That's all. I'll be perfectly safe. And then I'll be back with you in an hour, tops."

Cáel's jaw worked back and forth. "I don't like it."

I let out a breath. "Me neither. But we're going to get it over with so we can all move on."

Cáel leaned down, pressing his forehead to mine. "You tell me if they hurt you."

It wasn't a request.

"I'll tell you." But I knew the cops wouldn't hurt me physically. Emotionally was a whole other ball game.

Cillian made the turn onto campus, and my stomach pitched.

"They're at the science building. They're searching Brent's office," Maddox said.

Everything in me locked. "What if they find something from us?"

Maddox twisted in his seat. "We had enforcers clean it. There may be prints from you because you're his advisee, but we wiped clean the door and any other surfaces we might've touched. And we cleaned any blood evidence."

They had it all covered. A little *too* covered. It told me they'd done this before.

Cillian pulled into a parking spot behind the science building and turned to look at me. "Are you ready?"

My fingers were back together, tying themselves into those complex knots again. "I'm a really bad liar."

"You're not lying. You're telling the truth. You had a meeting with Brent. Knox picked you up from that meeting. When you left Brent, he was completely fine. Keep to the truth," Cillian said calmly.

I bit the inside of my cheek. I hoped his plan worked.

Cáel kissed my temple. "Be safe, Little One."

I bobbed my head. "I will."

Easton reached forward and squeezed my shoulder. "You've got this. Nice and easy."

"Thank you," I whispered. I was so nervous about the cops that I couldn't begin to think about Easton's affection.

Knox peeled my hands apart and linked his with one of mine. "Let's go, girlfriend."

He tugged me out of the SUV, then wrapped an arm around my shoulders. "An hour from now, this will all be over."

God, I hoped he was right.

Cillian and Maddox flanked us as we headed toward the science building. We were quiet as we walked.

Maddox held the door for us, and we moved inside. Classes were in session, so there weren't many students around, but the ones who were whispered as we passed. Great. Just great.

We all followed Maddox toward a conference room. The door was open, muted voices pouring out. As we stepped inside, two people looked up. Their expressions were hard to read. They had that same blank mask so many of the guys had perfected.

The woman stood first. She looked to be in her mid-forties with dark brown hair and a frame hidden by a suit that was just a size or so too big. "Mr. Kavanaugh, thank you for bringing in Hayden."

Maddox nodded. "Of course. Detective Brower, these are my brothers, Cillian and Knox. And this is Hayden."

The woman's gaze swept over all of us, assessing.

The man stood then. "We asked to speak to Hayden. Alone."

Cillian moved forward, extending his hand. "Cillian McCarthy. Since Hayden and Knox are living with me currently, I like to look out for them. Typically, I wouldn't let either of them speak to the police without a lawyer present, but since there's a missing person involved, I know how vital every moment is."

"Wouldn't *let* them?" the man challenged.

Brower shook her head. "Come on, Alwyn. It won't hurt anything to have them stay." She gestured to the conference table. "Please, have a seat."

Knox pulled out a chair for me, then took the one next to it. Cillian sat on my other side, and Maddox flanked Knox.

"So, Hayden, you are one of Professor Brent's advisees?" Brower asked.

I nodded. "Yes."

My voice sounded rusty even to my own ears.

"How do you like him?"

I stiffened, telling myself to breathe but stick to the truth. "He's not my favorite."

She arched a brow. "And why's that?"

I licked my lips. "More of a feeling, I guess. He can make me uncomfortable sometimes."

Knox took my hand, squeezing.

Brower was instantly on alert. "Has he ever touched you inappropriately?"

I was quiet for a moment, trying to choose my words carefully. "A hand on my thigh once."

She scribbled some notes down. "Did you report him?"

I shook my head. "I was just going to transfer advisors at the end of the term."

Alwyn huffed. "Sure, you were."

Brower sent him a scathing look. "How did Brent seem in your meeting yesterday?"

I squeezed Knox's hand so hard it would be a miracle if I didn't break any bones. "A little on edge, maybe? Upset."

Brower wrote more notes. "Did he tell you what he was doing after your meeting?"

"No, ma'am. But Knox showed up before he could end our meeting."

Her gaze flicked to Knox. "So, you saw Brent, as well?"

He nodded, looking perfectly cool and collected. "Hayden was late, so I knocked on the professor's door. I wanted to make sure I hadn't missed her."

"And how did Brent seem to you?" Brower asked.

Knox shrugged. "I don't really know the guy that well, but Hayden's right. He was on edge. Maybe annoyed that I'd shown up."

"And you two didn't see anyone else waiting to meet with him?" she pushed.

"Nope," Knox said easily. "Campus was pretty dead by then."

Brower took down a few more notes.

Alwyn pinned us with a stare. "Well, you two are the last people to see Professor Brent. So, you'll understand when we tell you not to leave town. You're both people of interest in his disappearance. And if you lied to us today, we *will* find out."

Chapter Forty-Six

Maddox

All color drained from Hayden's face at Detective Alwyn's words. Her already pale complexion was now a ghostly white, and I was pretty sure that if she hadn't been sitting, she'd have crumpled to the ground.

It took everything in me not to rip the man limb from limb. An image flashed in my mind of me punching into his chest. Of grabbing his heart and holding it while it still beat before ripping it from his chest.

Cillian pushed his chair back and stood. "It's a good thing they're college students and have classes to attend." His eyes narrowed on Alwyn, making the man swallow hard. "But since you've been so clear about where we stand with you, you'll understand that any future requests will be made through our lawyer."

He tossed a tiny scrap of paper onto the conference table. "There's his card."

Detective Brower glared at her partner. She was well aware that he'd fucked up royally. But if I had to guess, she was used to that.

Cillian motioned for Hayden and Knox to rise, and I followed suit as they stood. No one said a word as we headed out of the conference room and down the hall. More whispers surrounded us as classes let out, and I couldn't imagine how Hayden felt.

The moment we were outside, I breathed a little easier. Each inch of distance we got from that asshole had helped, too.

Knox wrapped Hayden in a hug. "Everything's going to be okay."

A wave of jealousy hit fast and hard. I wanted to hold her in my arms. Comfort her. Feel her heart beat against mine as her jasmine scent filled my nose. But that wasn't in the cards for me. Not anytime soon.

Cillian cleared his throat. "Do you want to head home?"

Hayden twisted in Knox's hold and shook her head. "I have English in a few minutes. I can't miss another class."

Cillian opened his mouth to argue, but Hayden cut him off with a shake of her head.

"It'll give me something to do besides obsess."

Knox shifted so that his arm was wrapped around her shoulders. "I'll walk you."

A muscle in Cillian's cheek fluttered. "Pete and Terry are waiting by the SUVs. Take them with you."

I was sure Cillian was battling the same things I was. All I wanted to do was get Hayden back to our territory, to our home, somewhere we could be assured of her safety.

Instead, we had to watch as Hayden and Knox walked away.

"We need to look into Alwyn," Cillian growled.

I didn't look away from Hayden's retreating form. "I already have the enforcers pulling background checks on him and Brower."

"Of course, you do," Cillian muttered. "Where did they dispose of the body?"

Finally, I forced my gaze to my alpha. "Deep into National Forest land. No one's going to find him. And if they do, it'll look like he was mauled by wild animals." Because he was, in a way. There was no one wilder than Cáel.

"Good." Cillian studied me carefully. "You have it together enough to get a feel for what the school knows?"

The muscles between my shoulder blades wound tighter. "I have it together," I gritted out.

Cillian simply looked at me in challenge. "You forget that I've known you almost half our lives. I know what you look like when you're fighting for control."

I ripped my gaze away from him, seeking out Hayden. She was small now, barely visible as she headed for the English building, Knox and the enforcers by her side.

"I failed her," I admitted. The words hurt to say out loud.

"We all did," Cillian said, emotion clogging his throat.

"But I worked with that bastard. If I hadn't been so concerned with keeping my distance from Hayden, I would've seen he was fixated on her."

Cillian's stare bored into me. "So, what does that mean for the future?"

My back teeth ground together. "That I'm sticking close."

"That's going to be hard for your dragon. He's going to be riding you hard to claim her, or at least to have physical closeness."

"I'll deal with it," I snapped. Even if it was pure agony.

I caught sight of a figure walking toward the science building. "That's the dean. I'll see what I can find out."

I didn't wait for Cillian's response. I simply strode toward the woman in her early fifties who wore her hair in an array of intricate braids. She looked like a woman on a mission, but she slowed as she saw me approach.

"Maddox. Have you met with them yet?"

No bullshit. Straight to the point. I admired that about Dean Robinson.

I nodded. "I did. They weren't all that forthcoming."

She huffed out a breath. "Of course, they weren't. They're disrupting my campus and scaring the hell out of my students. Paul probably just went on a bender."

Before I could speak, Dean Robinson held up a hand to stop me. "I shouldn't have said that. We should be doing everything we can to find him, even if he is an asshole."

I choked on a laugh. "Fair." The humor left me. "Have they told you *anything*?"

Dean Robinson shook her head. "Just that his wife reported him missing late last night when he didn't come home."

My brows hit my hairline. "Wife? I had no idea he was married."

Her mouth thinned. "I don't think Paul liked for that to be public knowledge."

"Creep," I muttered.

"You said it, not me." Dean Robinson sighed. "I'll need to find people to cover his classes and advisees."

"I can take one of his classes," I offered. "Just assign me one that fits into my schedule."

She patted my shoulder. "You're a godsend, Maddox. I'll do that. And you know the Parrish girl, right?"

I stiffened. "Yes. She's in my biology class, and she's dating Knox."

"Can you take her as an advisee? I'd like to place her with someone I know will be a good support after all of this."

My gut twisted. More time with Hayden. But better a little torture than having her with an unknown. "Sure. I'd be happy to."

"Thank you. I better go. Wouldn't want to keep the cops waiting."

Dean Robinson started on her way again, but I stayed rooted to the spot, wondering how the hell I was going to get through hours alone with Hayden without touching her.

Chapter Forty-Seven

Hayden

I curled into Cillian's side, letting his scent wrap around me. I'd never thought of smells as especially comforting before, but that all changed when I met the guys. The smoky cedar filling my senses was like a balm to my soul.

Cillian pulled me tighter against him. "You okay?"

I nodded as Knox took my feet into his lap and began massaging them.

"She's not okay," Cáel growled.

I sent him a pleading look. "Even if I'm not, can we just pretend that I am? Can we just play normal for one night?"

"Sure, we can," Cillian said and then paused. "What do normal people do on a weeknight?"

A laugh bubbled out of me and, God, it felt so damned good.

Cillian tickled my side. "Are you laughing at me?"

I squealed and smacked his thigh. "Stop it!" His tickling eased. "You have to admit, it's slightly amusing that you guys have no idea what normal is."

Knox kept kneading my foot. "Normal's overrated."

He had a point there.

A commotion sounded from the hallway, and everyone's gazes went to the family room door. Someone appeared, ladened down with pillows. But the stack was so high you couldn't see who it was. A second later, the figure dropped the huge pillows onto the floor.

"Uh, redecorating, East?" Knox asked, amusement in his voice.

"Just a sec," he said, hurrying back out.

A few moments later, he came in with a second heap of pillows. But he retreated before we could get any answers. Then he returned with his arms full of various bags.

Cáel arched a brow. "Preparing for the end of the world?"

"Maybe," Easton quipped. He turned to me, suddenly looking a little nervous.

He set the bags down on the coffee table and began pulling stuff out of them. There was kettle corn, cheddar popcorn, Red Vines, peanut butter M&M's, and root beer.

My heart started to beat faster. "Those are all my favorite snacks."

Easton shrugged. "Like I said, I pay attention."

I heard the message underneath his words. Easton was challenging my assumption that he didn't know me at all. Just because he hadn't been an active participant in conversations didn't mean that he wasn't hearing everything that was said.

I swallowed hard. "Thank you."

"What about my favorites?" Knox pouted.

Easton rolled his eyes, picking up another bag and tossing it at his brother. "I got your weird-ass favorites, too. I knew you wouldn't shut up if I didn't."

"Hey, pickle potato chips are *not* weird."

I scrunched up my nose. "That does sound a little gross."

Knox looked affronted.

Cáel chuckled. "Knox is like a pregnant woman with his snacks."

"Well, you assholes aren't getting any of my potato chips," Knox huffed.

"*Real* hardship," Cillian muttered.

Easton unloaded a bunch more stuff onto the coffee table that I assumed were Cillian's and Cáel's favorites.

"What are all the pillows for?" I asked.

He grinned at me. "Any good movie night needs a pillow fort."

My mouth curved in an answering smile. "I like a good pillow fort."

"See, all sorts of stuff in common." Easton handed me the remote. "The only thing I don't know is what kind of movies you like."

"Please don't make us watch *The Notebook*," Cáel muttered.

I glared at him. "Actually, horror movies are my favorite."

The guys all stilled.

Then Knox started laughing.

"What?" I demanded.

He struggled to get his words out. "Easton is a total scary-movie wimp."

Easton picked up a pillow and smacked his brother with it. "Shut up."

I pressed my lips together to keep from smiling. "What if I promise to protect you from the boogeyman?"

Tiny flecks of gold sparked in his eyes. "Gotta let me sleep with you tonight so he doesn't get me."

My stomach flipped. "Okay."

Easton's smile was back, and this time, it was a full-watt one. The effect was dazzling. It made his entire face light up. I was so very screwed.

I stood quickly. "I'll arrange the pillows."

I pushed the coffee table away from the couch so we'd have space as Cáel started listing off movie options.

"What about a classic?" I asked. "*The Exorcist*?"

Easton groaned. "That little girl is so fucking creepy."

I chuckled as I flopped down onto the pillows. "It's not her fault she got possessed by the devil."

He shivered as he lowered himself to the spot next to me. "They should've just killed her."

I gaped at him. "She was a little girl."

Easton shrugged, moving in closer to me. "Sacrifices must be made."

Cillian settled in on my other side. "He has a point."

I wanted to argue, but I was too distracted by their nearness. I hadn't gotten used to Easton's scent yet. That sea air with a hint of citrus. It was potent as hell and made me feel a little drunk.

I took a steadying breath. I could do this. Just two hours of my body going haywire.

Knox stood from the couch, crossing to turn off the lights. But he pulled up short as Maddox filled the door. "Hey, man."

Maddox looked exhausted. There were dark circles under his eyes and tension running along his shoulders. I had the sudden desire to launch up and give the man a hug.

"Want to watch a movie with us?" Easton offered.

Mad shook his head. "No, I'm going to get a little work done and then call it an early night."

Cillian shifted next to me. "Updates from the dean?"

Maddox shuffled his feet. "She doesn't know anything. Just asked me to take one of Brent's classes and an advisee or two." He cleared his throat, his gaze locking with mine. "Hayden, I'm your new advisor."

Everything in me locked. *Oh, shit.*

Chapter Forty-Eight

Hayden

The end credits rolled on the movie, but I barely saw them. *The Exorcist* was one of my favorite movies, but I'd hardly seen the film playing across the screen.

I'd been too distracted. Thinking about Maddox. Feeling the heat of Easton and Cillian next to me. Just knowing that I was surrounded by four of my mates.

My skin felt too tight for my body. My muscles felt twitchy, like I needed a good, long run. And I was *not* a runner.

Easton shifted, turning to me with a furrow in his brow. "You okay?"

I nodded my head slightly maniacally. "Yup. I'm good. Great. Thanks so much for a movie night."

The furrow only deepened. "You sure?"

"Yup." I clambered to my feet and started picking up detritus from the evening and stuffing it into an empty bag.

Knox sent Cillian a questioning look, but Cillian just shook

Knox sighed and got up. "I could use a workout. I've been cooped up too much today. Anyone want to fly or spar?"

Cillian rose. "We should stick close tonight. Let's spar."

I straightened and turned to Cillian. "You don't have to stick close because of me."

His mouth thinned. "There's a lot going on right now. The cops. The Corbetts. It would be better if we stuck together as much as possible."

My gaze dropped to the bag in my hands. I wanted to believe that Cillian's concern really was for all of us, but it was more likely that he was trying to protect my feelings.

Frustration flared. I didn't want to be the weak one. The one who couldn't properly protect herself.

I'd felt the animal within me stir as we'd flown this morning. I was ready for her to surface. God, I hoped she was fierce.

Easton got to his feet and gently took the bag from my hands. "I've got this."

I nodded. "Thanks. I'm going to get a little studying done."

I headed for the door before any of them could stop me. But I didn't head for my room. I went in search of Maddox.

He needed to know that he didn't have to be stuck with me. I could request a different advisor. I didn't want him to be forced into anything.

My bare feet padded along the floor. The only sound was them hitting hardwoods or rugs, depending on where I stepped. It didn't take long for me to reach Maddox's office.

The door was open, but the room was dark, no Maddox in sight. Still, I took a moment to take it all in. The light from the hall was enough to make out most things.

Like his bedroom, books dominated the walls. But there was less of a mix of genres here. The titles all seemed to have to do with science of some sort.

There was a tufted leather couch against one wall. The pillow on one side had a divot that made me think Maddox might nap there or at least recline while he read. I could picture it so easily, yet I couldn't paint his expression. The Maddox I'd seen was never completely relaxed.

He wore a mask that made it hard to tell what he was thinking, but that façade was always a touch formal. I wondered what it would look like to see him completely at ease, carefree even.

I frowned as I backed out of the space. To see that, Maddox would have to completely let down his shields around me. And that had only happened for brief moments at a time.

Heading back down the hallway, I made my way to the stairs. I took them two at a time, relishing the burn in my thighs. I moved toward Maddox's room and stopped at the closed door. Taking a deep breath, I knocked.

There was no answer.

I knocked again.

Nothing.

Annoyance flickered. Could he hear me and was just ignoring me?

I reached for the knob and twisted. Surprisingly, it was unlocked.

I opened the door to find the lights on but the room empty. I stepped further inside and frowned. There was no sign of him.

Finally, I heard the strains of water. I crossed to the bathroom door that was slightly ajar. I opened my mouth to call out but stopped dead as I caught sight of something in the mirror. Not some*thing* but some*one*.

Maddox's large frame was reflected in the mirror. His tanned skin pulled taut over defined muscles. Muscles that were bowed and flexed as he moved his hand up and down his shaft.

I needed to leave. Watching Maddox when he wasn't aware of my presence was beyond wrong. But I couldn't get my feet to move.

Maddox's fingers curled around himself, working his dick. Saliva filled my mouth as I wondered what he would feel like inside me. Moving in and out, thrusting deep.

My core convulsed with need.

Maddox tightened his hold on his cock as his hand picked up speed. He braced one hand on the tiled wall as he worked himself harder, faster.

My own breathing came quicker now as heat and wetness gathered between my thighs.

Maddox's mouth fell open as cum spurted against the wall. And there was only one word on his lips.

Hayden.

Chapter Forty-Nine

Hayden

The moment I heard my name on Maddox's lips, I bolted. Panic and heat raced through me. I never should've come into his bedroom when he didn't answer my knock, and I sure as hell shouldn't have looked in the bathroom. What was wrong with me?

I kept moving without really knowing where I was going. Until I heard the telltale sound of punching. Whether gloved fists were hitting bags or bodies, I didn't know. Not until I stepped into the room.

Some part of me had sought out my mates. Comfort in a moment of embarrassment and being turned way the hell on. Images of Maddox's hand around his cock, stroking, filled my head. The way his body had curved before he found his release. The way his lips had parted on my name.

But coming to the gym had been a massive mistake.

Cáel and Knox had been circling each other in a fight ring, but they stilled the moment I stepped inside. They wore nothing but workout shorts and hand wraps. Their feet were bare, and their muscled chests glistened with sweat. The sheen only made the definition clearer.

Knox's skin had that healthy golden hue that made me think of long summer days, while Cáel's was completely covered with ink. A skull dominated his torso. It was menacing but also beautiful. They were so different, yet equally beautiful.

Cillian pushed off the wall he leaned against, stalking toward me. He, too, was barefoot and bare chested. His massive form moved with catlike grace. "What's wrong?" he growled.

The blush on my cheeks deepened. "Nothing. Just, uh, wanted to see what you were up to. But you're busy."

I turned, about to bolt for the door, but Cillian caught my wrist. His hold managed to be both gentle and unyielding. "Little Flame…" he warned.

Slowly, I faced him, rolling my lips over my teeth.

He studied me carefully and then took a deep breath through his nose. "I smell anxiety and lust."

That had my blush fading and a glare taking its place. "Don't you think that little scent trick is a little invasive?"

"Not when it tells me what you're hiding from me. You're my mate. I need to know. What happened?"

I clamped my mouth closed as Cáel and Knox moved in closer.

"Hayden," Cillian crooned, his voice taking on a hypnotic lilt. His free hand dropped to my waist, squeezing. "Tell us."

I blamed whatever pheromones Cillian emitted for the word vomit that tumbled out of my mouth. "I went to find Maddox, but he was jerking off in the shower. I watched him, even though I should've left. And now I'm pretty sure I'm going to hell."

Knox's brows rose to his hairline. "Way to go, Mad."

Cáel smacked him. "You're not helping."

Cillian's lips twitched as his fingers traced designs on my side. "My Little Flame loves to watch."

My cheeks felt like they were burning. "I shouldn't have."

"I don't think Maddox would mind," Cillian said.

I shook my head. "I invaded his privacy."

Cillian studied me for a moment. "And now you're aching."

It wasn't a question, and I sure as hell wasn't about to admit to that.

He dropped his hold on my wrist, his fingers ghosting over the apex of my thighs.

It didn't matter that I was wearing sweatpants. I felt that touch like Cillian's fingers were skimming across my bare skin. Heat pooled low as my nipples pebbled against the cotton of my tank top.

"What do you need, Little Flame?" Cillian rasped. "Tell us and we'll give it to you."

My heart hammered harder against my ribs as Knox and Cáel moved even closer.

Cáel rounded me, sweeping the hair away from my neck and letting his lips skim from earlobe to shoulder. "Tell us, Little One."

My core constricted, pulsing with the need to be filled. I wanted to feel them filling me. Wanted their hands and mouths and cocks.

"I want everything," I whispered.

"Be. More. Specific," Cillian gritted out.

My eyes flashed. "You. All of you. Touching me. Making me come. Releasing all this need inside me."

It was then I realized just how desperate I was for them. I needed the intensity we shared to burn away everything that had happened over the past forty-eight hours. I wanted to forget. To lose myself in sensation. To push myself to the limits of what I could handle to remind myself I was alive.

Knox lifted a hand, palming my breast. "You heard her. Let's give our girl what she needs."

Hayden

My breath hitched as Knox circled my nipple through the thin cotton of my tank. I could feel the roughness of his fingertip even through the material. I wanted more. Needed more.

Cillian's eyes were hooded as his hand slipped under my tank. "Tell us now, Hayden. Soft and sweet or hard and claiming?"

Wetness gathered between my thighs. "Hard. Claiming."

My voice didn't sound like my own. It was raw with need. Desperate.

Cillian's eyes bled to black, and his finger squeezed my side. "Good answer. I've missed playing with my Little Flame."

A shiver racked through me. Not one of fear or discomfort but one of anticipation. My body knew the promise of what was to come.

Cáel sucked hard on my neck, and I knew he'd leave a bruise, but I didn't give a damn. The pull of his mouth on my skin had a mirroring sensation between my thighs.

"Cáel," I breathed.

He growled against my skin, sending tiny vibrations through me.

"Her shirt, Cáel," Cillian commanded.

A second later, I felt claws at the back of my neck. One hooked in my tank top and slid down in one fluid motion. The tearing sound filled the room.

Knox grabbed hold of the fabric and tossed it to the floor.

Cillian stared at my chest as if transfixed. "Knew those pretty little nipples were bare under there. Was staring at them all through the movie. Wanted to suck on them until you came fast and hard."

My breaths came quicker as Cillian leaned down and took a peak into his mouth. He didn't ease it in. He sucked hard and deep.

A strangled sound left my throat as my back arched, my head falling back against Cáel's chest.

Knox was on my other breast in a flash. His lips closed around my nipple, teasing and toying.

The sensations of Knox and Cillian were so different. The different tempos and techniques had my body going haywire.

"Please," I rasped.

"So beautiful when you beg," Cáel growled.

His arm came around me, his hand sliding into my sweats and panties. He let out a snarl. "Fucking soaked."

His fingers stroked me with ease, sending a new wave of sensation through me.

Cáel slid two fingers inside me as his thumb circled my clit.

"More," I demanded.

He added a third finger as Cillian's teeth grazed my nipple and Knox sucked deep.

I cried out, my orgasm coming fast and hard, nearly taking me to my knees.

Cáel's fingers pumped inside me, drawing out my shattering. There was so much feeling. Everywhere. All around me.

I struggled for breath as I came down, but Cillian had already dropped to his knees. He tugged off my sweats and panties, sending them flying. Then he was on his feet again. "Tell us we can have you," he gritted out.

There was only one answer. "I'm yours."

Cillian's shorts were gone in a flash, and I could feel Cáel press in behind me. His fingers dipped between my legs, gathering the wetness and spreading it over himself. Then his cock was nestling between my ass cheeks. My gaze flicked to the side as Knox bent, pulling his shorts free. His dick was hard, standing rigid against his belly.

How could I want all of them this much? It seemed like a physical impossibility. Yet there was no denying it. The need for each of them was a different color, a different texture. But each one was equally potent.

Cillian's large frame engulfed mine. "Tell me you're ready."

"Yes," I breathed.

He slammed into me. The force made my eyes water. Holy hell, it was everything I needed.

That desperation reminded me how wanted I truly was.

Cillian thrust in and out as Cáel's tip teased my ass. As Cill retreated, Cáel pushed in.

I cried out. So full. It was as if they were imprinting themselves on my very bones.

Knox stroked himself, a bead of pre-cum glistening on his tip.

I needed him, too. Was desperate for him.

I reached out a hand, taking his length and stroking.

Cillian growled low. "Tell me you're mine."

"I'm yours. All of yours."

His eyes were black again as he thrust impossibly deeper. Tears leaked out of my eyes with the force of sensation. Cáel met him thrust for thrust.

Cillian's canines elongated. "I can feel him pushing me out, demanding I take you deeper."

"Please," I begged.

Cillian's throat worked as he swallowed. "Ready to be fully mine?"

I knew what it meant. The mate bite. The bond cementing.

Want, need, and love all swirled inside me. "Yes. Love you, Cill."

I knew he couldn't say it back, knew he didn't trust himself to know what it meant. But I knew this was the path to showing him.

"You're everything to me." Cillian thrust inside, his teeth sinking into my shoulder.

Cáel pushed deeper from behind as my hand tightened around Knox. I cried out so loudly, I swore people would be able to hear my screams from miles around. Pleasure rippled through me, so intense it bordered on pain.

I squeezed the life out of all of them, my core and ass tightening, my hand pumping Knox faster. Cillian sucked on my claiming mark, only heightening my pleasure. Nonsensical words left my lips as my orgasm rocked through me.

Then my own teeth were lengthening, something inside me telling me to bite, to claim Cillian for my own. I moved on instinct, sinking my teeth into his neck and making him come so hard I felt the pulse inside me.

Cáel shouted out his release just as Knox did the same.

All of us, falling apart and coming together.

My teeth retracted as I struggled to stay on my feet.

Cáel's arm came around my waist, holding me up. "Never felt anything so beautiful."

I looked up into Cillian's eyes as his dick twitched inside me.

"Everything," he said and then brushed his lips against mine.

I shuddered, and both Cillian and Cáel groaned.

Knox dropped a kiss to my shoulder as I released him. "Gonna get a towel to clean you up."

That had my cheeks heating as he bent to grab a towel from the stack on the bench behind us. He wiped his release from my stomach as Cillian and Cáel pulled out. I couldn't help the wince.

Cillian's hand ghosted over my cheek, so much reverence there. "Tender?"

"Just a little."

"Need to get you into the bath."

That sounded heavenly.

Cillian lifted me into his arms, and I burrowed into his hold. But as he turned for the door, he came up short.

Easton stood there, eyes a fiery gold. He'd been watching. Everything.

Chapter Fifty-One

Hayden

The sunlight streamed in through the window as I watched Cillian sleep. His face was so relaxed. It was the first time I'd seen him completely at ease. Each exhale of breath made his lashes flutter, and my fingers itched to touch him.

I could feel him now. Just like I could feel Cáel and Knox, who lay behind me. I could feel the sense of peace they all had at being bonded. And it eased something in me, too. Let me dare to hope.

"You're staring, Little Flame," Cillian said without opening his eyes.

I grinned. "How do you know?"

"I can feel it." His eyes fluttered open. "And I can feel that you're happy."

"I am," I told him honestly.

"I'd be happier if we could sleep another hour," Knox mut-

Cáel chuckled as he flopped to his back. "You can take a nap later."

Cillian traced the bite mark on my shoulder. The contact had heat sparking. He smiled then. "Love that I can feel your want, your need."

"Makes sex that much more awesome," Knox mumbled. "It's like her pleasure stokes ours."

He was so right about that. I looked at my shoulder. The bite mark was still raw, but below it had formed a tiny tree with arching branches. "It's beautiful. What does it mean?"

Cillian traced the brand. "I think it has to do with my gift."

I frowned. "What is it?"

"I can blend in with my surroundings in dragon form. It's like I become invisible against the trees and sky."

"I better get a cool gift," I groused.

Cillian chuckled. "I have no doubt."

"I want to see my mark—" My words cut off as I remembered that I'd bitten him on the neck. Somewhere the entire world would be able to see. My hand flew to my mouth. "Oh, shit. Cillian. I'm so sorry. I shouldn't have bitten you on the neck. I wasn't thinking—"

Cillian leaned forward, kissing me. "I love that my mark will be where everyone can see it."

"But the wound. Isn't that going to be a little suspicious?"

The last thing we needed was more questions right now.

Cillian rolled to his back, exposing his neck.

My jaw went slack. It was completely healed. There was only the faint scar and the gemstone beneath it.

"Alpha show-off," Knox chided.

I glanced at him in question.

"Dragons who are able to shift heal way faster than humans, but alphas heal even faster," Knox explained.

I turned back to Cillian, tracing the scar with my finger.

He shuddered. "Careful, Little Flame."

I tugged my hand back. "Sorry."

Cillian grinned. "Don't be, but I don't think you're up for another round this morning."

I still felt Cillian's and Cáel's presence between my legs and backside. As much as I wanted to, I probably needed a day to recover.

Cillian laughed then. The sound was so uninhibited it hit me right in the chest. "Love that you're pouting about not being up for sex."

I smacked his chest. "Shut up."

He hauled me against him. "How about breakfast instead?"

"That's a sad fucking substitute," Knox griped.

Cáel pushed up against the pillows, grinning. "You know you have him wrapped around your finger when he'd pick you over food, Little One."

Knox leaned over and nipped my bottom lip. "You taste better than cinnamon rolls."

Shit. If I didn't get out of this bed, we were all definitely going to fuck.

Quickly, I rolled over Cillian. "Out. All of you. I don't trust myself around all your crazy dragon pheromones."

They all laughed, but I made a beeline for my bathroom, closing and locking the door behind me. Like that would do any good. They could knock that door in with a flick of their pinky.

I leaned against the wood, taking a deep breath. "I'm becoming a sex-crazed maniac."

"And we like you that way," Knox yelled.

"Damned shifter hearing," I groused. "Get out of my room!"

More laughter sounded from the other room.

I pushed off the door, flipping them off, even though they couldn't see me. It was the principle of the matter. If I wasn't such a needy hussy, I'd give them blue balls for a week.

I made quick work of brushing my teeth and washing my face, cursing dragons and their magic dicks the whole time. By the time I was done with that, said dragons had thankfully fled my room. I crossed the closet, pulling out jeans, a blouse, and a sweater. While Cáel's and Knox's claiming marks were beginning to fade, Cillian's was still fresh. I'd have to be wary of what I wore for the next few days at least. Thankfully, the fall weather made it easier to cover up.

Dressing quickly in my now-typical collared shirt, I pulled my hair back into a braid and grabbed my backpack. As I made my way out of my bedroom and toward the stairs, my steps slowed. I couldn't help but wonder if Easton would be at breakfast.

He'd taken off without a word last night, but I'd seen the longing in his eyes, the hurt even. It made my stomach twist in a vicious cramp. I wanted to believe that he'd changed his view of me, but I couldn't quite get myself to fully let go.

Forcing myself to keep going, I headed for the dining room. All the guys were there but Maddox. My gaze instantly went to Easton, who had yet again taken Knox's seat next to mine.

As our eyes locked, he pulled out my chair. It was a tiny gesture, but it told me he wasn't harboring any negative emotions. I let out the breath I'd been holding and headed for the seat.

I lowered myself into the chair, scooting in. Then I reached under the table and squeezed his hand.

Easton's gaze flew to my face.

I couldn't give him everything he wanted just yet. But I could give him this.

The smile that spread across his face was a punch to the gut. He squeezed my fingers and then released them. "Scrambled eggs, pancakes, or both?"

"Uh," I began, still trying to find words after seeing the sheer joy on Easton's face.

"She wants both," Cáel answered for me.

I turned to him and stuck out my tongue. "Interfering dragon."

He just grinned at me.

Footsteps sounded in the hallway, and we all turned to see Maddox stride into the room. There was no hint of amusement on his face.

"What's wrong?" Cillian demanded.

His mouth thinned. "The police found Brent's body."

Chapter Fifty-Two

Cillian

I paced back and forth in my office as Maddox stood sentry. "There's no way they should've known where that body was."

Maddox's teeth ground together. "No, there's not."

"Who from our horde knew where it was?" I demanded.

Maddox stiffened. "You're thinking we have a traitor?"

"Do you have any better ideas?" The idea had my gut tightening in a painful twist. We'd already had a human employee let the Corbetts into my club. But this would be an entirely different kind of betrayal.

"All the enforcers knew," Maddox said quietly. "They may have told partners or friends. We didn't demand it be kept secret."

And why would we? We trusted our people. But unless the Corbetts or the cops had managed drone surveillance without our knowledge, this was the only option.

I scrubbed a hand over my stubbled jaw. "We need to figure this out, and fast."

Maddox jerked his head in a nod. "Cops are going to want to talk to Hayden again."

My hands fisted as my beast rose to the surface. He wouldn't want anyone near Hayden after claiming her, but people who might wish her harm? That would be a recipe for disaster.

Maddox studied me for a moment. "Can you keep your dragon in check?"

"Yes," I ground out. But I wasn't so sure.

Maddox read that and cursed. "We call in the lawyer."

"It's going to take him hours to get here. Even if he takes the jet." Our overpriced shark worked out of San Francisco, so it wasn't like his office was around the corner.

"Let's get him on the way, just in case they make the request."

I nodded. "Call him."

A knock sounded on my door. "Come in."

Easton eased it open. "We're all ready to go. You guys coming with?"

My body was moving before my mouth could answer. I couldn't imagine letting Hayden go to campus without me. Not when we didn't know who we could trust, and the cops could still be combing the place.

"We're coming," I bit out.

Easton simply nodded and headed back toward the foyer. Maddox and I followed behind him.

Hayden was waiting in the entryway, bracketed by Cáel and Knox. As if by sticking close, they could ease the anxiety thrumming through her. Even if I hadn't been able to smell it lacing the air, it would've been as clear as day. She wrung her hands over and over, her skin pale.

I crossed the space, taking her face in my hands. "We're not going to let anything happen to you."

"I know," she whispered.

Such unwavering faith.

Hayden looked up into my eyes. "How did they know?"

That sinking feeling was back. "I don't know. But I'm sure as hell going to find out."

She worried a spot on the inside of her cheek. "I don't want any of you to get in trouble."

Knox scoffed. "Never going to happen."

God, I hoped he was right. I'd never had the cops paying this close attention before. At least the shed was hidden deep on our property. It would take days, possibly weeks, for the cops to search our land, even if they could get a search warrant. Still, I'd need to make sure it had been cleansed of all evidence of Brent.

We'd need an extra dose of hydrogen peroxide. The only thing that could truly be trusted to clean all remnants of blood. Add that to the list.

I brushed my lips across Hayden's forehead. "Let's get you to school."

Her eyes widened. "You're coming?"

I nodded. "I'll chill in Mad's office. But I want to be close."

It would kill me not to be by her side. But I'd just have to trust my brothers to stick close.

Hayden's shoulders relaxed a fraction. "It helps, knowing you'll be there."

Warmth spread through me, eating away at some of the fear. Was that sensation love? I hated that I hadn't given Hayden the words. But I wouldn't lie to her. Not to my mate. My childhood had left me unequipped to truly know what that emotion was. It had never been safe for me to experience it.

But for the first time, I wanted to give it to someone. To *Hayden*.

"We need to go," Maddox said quietly.

I nodded, leading the way out to the SUV. I motioned for Maddox to take the wheel. I needed to be close to Hayden. Needed to feel her.

My dragon was riding me hard. He wanted to scoop her up and hide her in a cave on the mountain. And part of me didn't disagree.

Instead, I climbed into the vehicle and hauled her onto my lap. Hayden looked up at me, puzzled.

I pressed a kiss to the corner of her mouth as the rest of the guys piled into the SUV. "Need as much of you as I can have before we get there."

Knox glanced at us from the seat behind. "His dragon's going to be extra possessive, since the bond is so new."

"Oh," Hayden said, sympathy filling her tone as Maddox started the SUV. She burrowed into me, giving me the contact I so desperately needed.

"Thank you," I rasped.

"It's not exactly a hardship cuddling you, Cill."

Cáel chuckled next to us. "What about me?"

Hayden grinned. "You either."

He took her legs and spread them over his lap, kneading her calves through her jeans. "Good."

The ride to campus was quiet after that. We were all lost in our own worlds of worry and what-ifs, but my dragon was soothed by his mate's scent and the beat of her heart against ours.

As Maddox pulled into a parking spot by the science building, I brushed my lips against Hayden's. "Stay close to the guys today, okay?"

She nodded.

Easton twisted in his seat. "We have bio and psych this morning, so I'll be with her the whole time."

That eased some of the panic flowing through me. "Good."

Hayden kissed the underside of my jaw. "We've got this."

I nodded but didn't say a word.

Finally, Cáel opened his door. We all took it as a sign to get out.

Hayden followed behind me, but we pulled up short as two figures strode toward us.

Detective Alwyn glared at Hayden. "Ms. Parrish. We need to speak with you. *Now.*"

Chapter Fifty-Three

Hayden

My throat stuck as I tried to swallow. Knox instantly moved to my side, wrapping an arm around me and pulling me in. "Not without her lawyer."

Detective Alwyn's eyes narrowed on me. "You have something to hide, Hayden?"

"No," Cillian clipped. "But after your unprofessional display yesterday, it was clear we needed our lawyer on hand for all conversations. He is on his way, but Hayden won't be speaking to you without him present."

"You let them control you?" Alwyn challenged.

Cillian stiffened. "Keep talking and I'll be lodging a formal complaint with the police department and the mayor. I have *very* deep ties to this town. Remember that."

Alwyn's face reddened, and he opened his mouth to say something, but Detective Brower held up her hand to stop him. "Enough." She turned to Cillian. "My apologies. My partner is understandably upset. After an anonymous tip, we found Mr. Brent in pieces deep in National Forest territory. It was quite unsettling."

My stomach pitched, and I turned into Knox. But I didn't miss how Brower was watching us. All of us. She wanted to drop that bomb to see our reactions.

Cillian's face remained a blank mask. "That would be quite upsetting."

Brower nodded slowly. "So, you'll understand why it's important for us to find answers."

"As long as that quest follows *legal* pathways, I support it wholeheartedly," Cillian said coolly.

"Glad to hear it." Brower turned to me. "Be at the precinct at nine tomorrow morning with your lawyer." Her gaze flicked to Cáel. "You, too."

I stiffened in Knox's hold, but it was Maddox who spoke. "Why do you need to speak with Cáel?"

Brower smiled at him, but it wasn't in any way warm. "We have an eyewitness who put him in the building at the time Brent was last seen. I'm assuming he'd like a lawyer present, as well, so we'll get this all done at once. Unless you'd like to get it over with now, Mr. McKenna?"

"No, he wouldn't," Cillian growled.

The detective turned her smile on Cillian. "Then we'll just keep going with our investigation until then. Remember, you'll need to stay in town."

Alwyn gave us one last glare, and then they both turned to walk away.

"This is bad," Easton muttered.

A muscle in Cillian's jaw fluttered. "I'll deal with it."

Knox glanced at him. "We're sure there's nothing on the body that would tie it to Cáel or to our property?"

Cillian shook his head. "You know we always take precautions."

"Murder cases have been made on circumstantial evidence before," Easton said quietly.

"Not with the legal team we have," Maddox assured him.

I crossed to Cáel, wrapping my arms around his waist and

holding on. I didn't care who saw or what they thought. I needed to comfort him. To reassure myself that he was here and safe.

Cáel's arms came around me. "I'll be fine, Little One. Been in worse jams than this one before."

I hated that with every fiber of my being.

Maddox cleared his throat. "We need to get to class or there will be more talk."

I nodded against Cáel but didn't let him go.

He dipped his head and brushed his lips over my hair. "Go to class. I'll be waiting for you after."

I forced myself to release my hold on him, stepping back.

Easton lifted my backpack, offering it to me.

I slid it over my shoulder and followed him and Maddox toward the science building, leaving the rest of the guys to problem solve.

The moment we stepped inside the building, the whispers intensified.

"They think *she* killed him."

"I heard she was fucking him, too, and got pissed when she found out he was married."

"No, they're all part of a satanic cult, and Brent was a sacrifice."

I tried to tune it out, but the words slammed into me one after the other. But the one that I was stuck on the most was that Professor Brent had been *married*. What a sleazy creep. That was probably wrong to say about the dead, but it was the truth.

Easton moved in closer to me, his shoulder brushing mine. "You okay?"

"Everything's just sunshine and roses."

He winced. "Cillian has gotten us out of worse situations than this one. It'll be ugly for a couple of weeks, and then it will stop."

I wasn't so sure about that. It wasn't as if they were going to find the real killer and our names would be cleared. Because we had killed him.

I included myself in that *we* because I'd been the instigator. The guys were protecting *me*.

Maddox led us into his biology classroom, heading for his desk. The room was already full of students who were whispering quietly. I headed down the row toward my table at the back.

I didn't even notice Delaney until I heard her.

"It was bad enough when you were a manipulative slut, but now you're a murderer. God, just get expelled already."

The students around her broke into laughter or gasps.

"Enough," Maddox snapped. His eyes narrowed on Delaney. "Do I need to report you to the dean for harassment?"

Her cheeks flamed. "I'm sorry, Professor, but I don't feel safe with a suspected murderer in our midst."

I quickly ducked into my seat next to Wren.

"That's it," Maddox said, his voice practically vibrating. "Please leave my class. You can get the notes from a fellow student if anyone can stand to be in proximity to your vitriol."

Delaney's jaw dropped open. "You can't do that."

Maddox arched a brow. "I can't? It's an absence or a meeting with Dean Robinson. Your choice."

Delaney leapt out of her chair, shoving her books into her bag and stomping down the aisle.

"She looks like a two-year-old throwing a tantrum," Wren muttered.

I wanted to smile, but I couldn't quite get my lips to curve. The imagery was right on the money, but there was too much weighing on me to truly let the joke land.

Wren lowered her voice as Maddox began his lecture. "Are you all right?"

I glanced over at Wren, her dark brown hair falling in her face. "Not really."

"I'm so sorry. Everyone knows Brent was a dick of the greatest proportions." She glanced around to see if anyone was listening.

"I heard he's taken advantage of students before, maybe worse. It's not some big loss."

My stomach twisted. I'd been right; there were others. I chose my words carefully before giving voice to them. "He wasn't a good man."

Wren reached under the table and squeezed my hand. "Then he got what he deserved."

She was right. If Brent had been doing this to woman after woman, he'd earned his fate.

I tried to focus on Maddox's words for the rest of class, but it was a struggle. By the time the bell rang, I thought only half of the words had made it into my brain.

I gathered my stuff and followed Easton and Wren out of the classroom. Easton pulled out his phone, frowning at the screen. "Knox said to meet him and the guys in the quad."

"Okay." I glanced at Wren. "What do you have next?"

"Photography. Across campus," she answered as we stepped out into the sunshine.

I caught sight of Cillian, Cáel, and Knox near some tables. They were talking to another guy. He was huge, nearly the size of Cillian. His dark brown hair was almost black and hung long around his shoulders. His eyes were a piercing blue-green, and next to one of them was a tattoo of a knife.

Wren stilled next to me, her body going completely rigid.

I slowed, turning to face her. "Are you okay?"

"I-I have to go."

She bolted away from us. But it was in the opposite direction of her class.

Hayden

I watched as Wren wound through students, disappearing at just short of a run. I frowned as I turned back toward the guys, again taking in the stranger.

"Is that your *lawyer*?" I whispered to Easton.

He barked out a laugh. "Hell no. Our lawyer is in his fifties with a paunch and a three-hundred-dollar haircut."

That definitely made more sense. "Then, who is that?"

Easton shifted his weight on his feet, losing any sign of amusement.

"East?" I probed.

"It's Brix," Maddox said, coming up beside me.

I looked up at him, silently asking for more information.

"He's a new contact of Cillian's," Maddox explained.

"Be honest, Mad. He's a mercenary. He gets paid to do less-than-legal things," Easton cut in.

A flicker of nerves took root in my belly. "Why does Cillian need him now?"

Maddox met my eyes. "He and his wolf pack, the Diablos, have been looking into your parents' deaths."

"What?" I croaked.

"They have resources we don't. They're very good at finding information no one else can," Maddox said calmly.

"But at what price?" If someone was a mercenary, then they weren't going to simply do us a kindness.

Easton squeezed my arm. "Don't worry. Cill is paying them well."

I hated that, too. I didn't want Cillian to have to spend more money on me.

"It's nothing to him, Mo Ghràidh," Maddox said softly. "A drop in the bucket."

I nodded, but it didn't change how I felt.

Maddox placed a hand on my back, gently guiding me forward.

As we walked up to the group, the stranger's eyes were on me. Assessing. As if he were looking for any signs of weakness.

I swallowed hard and extended my hand. "Hi. I'm Hayden."

The man stared down at my hand, not taking it.

Cillian cleared his throat. "Brix doesn't shake hands."

I quickly pulled my hand back. "Sorry."

Brix's gaze flicked over my shoulder. "The girl you were talking to. Who is she?"

I frowned. "Just a friend."

"Name," he commanded.

Easton rolled his eyes. "Chill. She's a human classmate."

Brix's eyes narrowed on East. "I decide what's important."

"Her name is Wren," I cut in, trying to defuse the situation. "We have a few classes together, but I don't know her super well. She's nice and shy. Definitely hasn't tried to slit my throat or anything."

The man's lips thinned. He was silent for a moment, completely unworried about filling the quiet or having awkward pauses in conversation. Finally, his focus came back to me. "Do you remember living anywhere other than Maine?"

I twisted my fingers together, pulling them taut. I tried not to think about my childhood often. It hurt too much to remember all I'd lost. "No. My first memories are of that house."

"Do you remember ever seeing your parents shift or show any abilities that seemed inhuman?" Brix pressed.

"No." Everything about my life and my parents' lives had been so very normal. Right up until that awful night.

"Tell me what happened when they were killed."

My knuckles blanched white as my stomach bottomed out.

"No," Knox clipped. "She doesn't have to go through that."

Brix pinned Knox with a stare that would've made me piss myself. "Do you want to know what happened to her family or not?"

"You can do it another way," Knox gritted out. "I thought you guys were the best of the best. But maybe the rumors are exaggerated."

Brix let out a low growl.

"I can do it," I said quickly. The last thing we needed in the middle of campus was a brawl.

Taking a deep breath, I steeled myself. I tried to get all the words out without letting the memories land. "I was staying up past my bedtime, reading. I heard footsteps in the hallway. My mom barreled into my room and pulled me out of bed. She told me to hurry. She made me hide in this attic space I never knew about. But I could hear what was going on below."

Pain streaked through me as I heard the voices as though it had been yesterday. "Some men came in. They spoke to my mom in another language, but I could tell they were threatening. They kept asking where *she* was. Then they killed her."

I could still see all the blood, feel it beneath my hands as I tried to save her. Tears filled my eyes, and Cáel wrapped an arm around my shoulders, pulling me into him.

"Enough," he barked.

Brix barely spared him a glance. "Do you remember anything that was said in the other language?"

I shivered against Cáel. "*Càit a bheil a' bhana-phrionnsa??*"

Brix went rigid, his blue-green eyes sparking.

"What?" Cillian demanded. "That means something to you?"

"Don't know for sure yet," Brix clipped.

"Tell us what you *think,* then. We thought it might mean that her mother was running from an abusive relationship. Lots of fathers call their daughters princess."

"Maybe," Brix said low. "I need to go. I'll be in touch."

And with that, he was gone.

Knox glared at Cillian. "You still think using them is a good idea?"

Cillian gritted his teeth. "They're the best at finding information, even if their methods are unorthodox."

But something told me that Brix already knew something. He just wasn't ready to share that information.

CHAPTER FIFTY-FIVE

Hayden

I SLID MY BOOKS INTO MY BACKPACK AS CÁEL AND EASTON hovered nearby. It felt like this day had actually lasted a month. And to top it all off, I was worried about Wren. She had missed English. And as far as I knew, she'd never missed class a day in her life.

I wanted to text her, but I realized I didn't have her phone number. Some friend I was. I'd been so caught up in the craziness of the last couple of months that I hadn't even bothered to get it. I'd send her an email as soon as we got home.

The moment I zipped up my backpack, Cáel picked it up.

"You don't have to—"

He cut me off with a droll look.

"Alrighty then," I mumbled.

"Let him do it. Makes him feel useful when everything is literal chaos around us," Easton said.

He was right. We all needed to hold tight to anything that would give us some semblance of control.

I moved into Cáel's space, stretching up and pressing a kiss to the underside of his jaw. "Thank you."

Cáel just grunted, but it made me smile.

"Let's get out of here," Easton muttered. "I need a stiff drink and ten hours in the hot tub."

I chuckled. "I wouldn't be against that. Where's Maddox?"

"He's waiting at the car," Easton explained.

Cillian and Knox were already home, crafting a plan of attack with the lawyer for our meeting tomorrow. Suddenly, going home seemed more exhausting than staying put.

Easton wrapped an arm around me. "It won't be too bad. Promise."

I just hoped he was right.

We headed through the maze of hallways toward the back door. As we turned a corner, we nearly collided with Delaney, Bella, and Maggie.

Delaney sneered at me. "If it isn't the slutty murderer. Did you slice and dice Brent yourself, or did you offer one of these two a blow job to do it?"

A snarl left Cáel's lips, making all three girls stumble back a few steps. Bella and Maggie kept retreating, but Delaney stood her ground.

"What? Are you going to kill me, too? There are witnesses, you know," she snapped.

"Delaney," Bella hissed.

Maggie just shook her head. "This is too much for me. I am so out."

Delaney whirled on them. "Shut up. I will ruin both of you."

Maggie's cheeks went pink. "You're obsessed with Hayden, and it's getting really fucking weird. So, she snagged the guy you're interested in. It's not like there aren't hundreds more on campus to choose from. Get over it already."

Redness crept up Delaney's throat. "You have no idea what you're talking about."

Bella gaped at her. "It's all you talk about now. You pick apart everything about Hayden, practically accuse her of wanting to wear your skin."

I wrinkled my nose at that. *No, thank you.*

Delaney fisted her hands. "Excuse me for not wanting a *murderer* at our school."

Maggie rolled her eyes. "You don't care about that. All you care about is Knox. Or maybe it's Cillian. It's hard to keep up with you."

"You're both done," Delaney snarled.

Bella held up a hand. "Please, everyone knows you're the one who's losing it. Good luck starting *more* rumors."

Bella motioned to Maggie, and they took off back down the hall.

Easton cleared his throat. "You going to be done with this weird-ass war against Hayden now?"

Delaney turned back around slowly, her teeth gritted. But she didn't look at Easton. Her hate-filled eyes were only locked on me. "You are going to pay for this."

She strode forward, shoulder-checking me as she passed.

I sighed. "I don't think the loss of friends got through to her."

Cáel grunted. "She needs some serious help."

"Not going to argue with you there," I muttered.

Easton wrapped an arm around my shoulders. "Let's get home."

If there wasn't a lawyer waiting for us there, that would've sounded perfect.

As we stepped outside, Maddox pushed off the SUV. "Where have you been? I was about to come looking for you."

"Little mean-girl run-in," Easton answered.

Maddox's gaze flicked to me. "Delaney?"

I nodded. "Not my biggest fan."

He groaned. "Maybe I need to get the dean involved."

I shook my head. "It'll just make things worse. I can deal with her insults. At some point, it just becomes background noise."

Maddox held my gaze for a moment, as if trying to read the truth behind my words. "You'll tell me if it gets to be too much?"

"I promise." But given everything else we were facing, I could deal with Delaney.

"All right. Let's get home. Cillian's getting antsy," Maddox said, beeping the locks on the SUV.

He and Easton climbed into the front while Cáel and I got into the back. We were all mostly quiet as Maddox drove. There were a million worries to dominate our thoughts, and no one was in the mood for music.

Maddox turned onto the two-lane road that led toward horde territory. At least there I wouldn't be quite so on edge. Until the lawyer started peppering me with questions that was.

I needed ice cream. A vat of it. With chocolate syrup and whipped cream. And sprinkles. All the rainbow sprinkles.

The sound of an engine was the only warning. It was a puzzling noise because there were no other vehicles in sight. By the time I was looking around to find the source, it was too late.

Something slammed into our SUV, sending it flipping over and off the road. It tumbled several times before stopping upside down.

Everything and nothing hurt all at the same time. My ears rang as a warm liquid dripped down the side of my face. Blood, some part of my brain registered.

Someone groaned from the front seat as voices shouted from outside the vehicle.

What the hell happened?

"Cut her down. The alpha's gonna be pissed if she's dead," a man yelled.

"Hayden?" Easton croaked from the front seat, his voice barely audible.

Hands reached in through the smashed-out window, and a knife glinted.

Panic set in, and I kicked out.

The man cursed, grabbing me by the hair. "Don't make me gut you."

"Hayden!" Easton yelled, trying to get out of his seat belt. I saw a flash of claws, and he cut himself free. But just as quickly, a pop sounded, making Easton's body jerk.

"Hayden..." he choked, slumping against the SUV's roof.

The hand tightened in my hair as I thrashed. I screamed for Maddox and Cáel, but they didn't wake up. Or they were already dead. *No.* They weren't. I'd have felt it.

I fought harder, kicking out and screaming. The man cursed again, and then there was a sharp pinch in my neck. Just as quickly as I'd felt the bite of pain, it was fading. And with it, the world around me.

Hayden's story comes to an end in *Dawn of Flames.*

Also by Tessa Hale

Dragons of Ember Hollow

Twilight of Embers

Midnight of Ashes

Dawn of Flames

Supernaturals of Castle Academy

Legacy of Shadows

Anchor of Secrets

Destiny of Ashes

Royals of Kingwood Academy

The Lost Elemental

The Last Aether

The Queen of Quintessence

The Shifting Fate Series

Spark of Fate

Mark of Stars

Bond of Destiny

Connect With Tessa

You can find Tessa at various places on the internet.
These are her favorites...

Website
www.tessahale.com

Newsletter
www.tessahale.com/newsletter

Facebook Page
bit.ly/TessaHaleFB

Facebook Reader Group
bit.ly/TessaHaleBookHangout

Instagram
www.instagram.com/tessahalewrites

Goodreads
bit.ly/TessaHaleGR

BookBub
www.bookbub.com/authors/tessa-hale

Amazon
bit.ly/TessaHaleAmazon

About Tessa Hale

Author of love stories with magic, usually with more than one love interest. Constant daydreamer.

Made in United States
Troutdale, OR
04/11/2024

19089426R00152